Wildlife
according to
Og the Frog

Look for all of the adventures in Room 26

Don't miss Betty G. Birney's chapter books for younger readers

Wildlife

according to

Og the Frog

Betty G. Birney

putnam

G. P. Putnam's Sons

G. P. Putnam's Sons
An imprint of Penguin Random House LLC, New York

Copyright © 2020 by Betty G. Birney

G. P. Putnam's Sons is a registered trademark of Penguin Random House LLC.

Visit us online at penguinrandomhouse.com

Library of Congress Cataloging-in-Publication Data
Names: Birney, Betty G., author.
Title: Wildlife according to Og the frog / Betty G. Birney.
Description: New York: G. P. Putnam's Sons, [2020] | Series: Og the frog; book 3 |
Summary: "Og the frog goes to summer camp with his best pal Humphrey, and has an exciting adventure in the wild"—Provided by publisher.
Identifiers: LCCN 2019029818 (print) | LCCN 2019029819 (ebook) |
ISBN 9781984813756 (hardcover) | ISBN 9781984813763 (ebook)
Subjects: CYAC: Camps—Fiction. | Adventure and adventurers—Fiction. | Frogs—Fiction. | Hamsters—Fiction. | Forest animals—Fiction.
Classification: LCC PZ7.B5229 Wil 2020 (print) | LCC PZ7.B5229 (ebook) | DDC [Fic]—dc23
LC record available at https://lccn.loc.gov/2019029818
LC ebook record available at https://lccn.loc.gov/2019029819

Printed in the United States of America
ISBN 9781984813756
1   3   5   7   9   10   8   6   4   2

Design by Eileen Savage | Text set in Warnock Pro

To Cynthia, Jeanne, Michelle, Merelyn and the indomitable Marian

CONTENTS

The End

· · · · · · · · · · · · · · · · ·

*In the swamp, the only thing
that stays the same is change.*

—Granny Greenleaf's
Wildlife Wisdom

I can't believe it's happening to me again!

Just a few months ago, I was frognapped out of my home in the swamp—the only home I've ever known. I went from a life full of my lively green frog friends, classes with our teacher, the wise Granny Greenleaf, all the yummy insects a frog could dream of and long afternoons floating on a lily pad to my new life at Longfellow School.

The human world was strange at first, but I came to like the big tads in Mrs. Brisbane's class. I even became friends with a furry fellow whose cage is next to my tank. Humphrey is his name, and he's the other classroom pet in Room 26.

Now, just as I've learned the ins and outs of being a classroom frog and have come to love this new life, it's over! Gone!

And I have no idea what comes next.

It all begins on a warm day, when I am gazing out the window at the blue sky. Our teacher, Mrs. Brisbane, suddenly says, "Just four days until the end of school."

I am as shocked as a bat in bright light!

I'd think I didn't hear her correctly, except for the fact that Humphrey also squeaks in alarm.

"SQUEAK-SQUEAK-*SQUEAK*!" he cries out. He's a squeaky little hamster, but he has a big heart.

"I can't believe it!" I say, even though I know Humphrey and the big tads only hear the twangy sound I make: "BOING-BOING!" They think it's funny.

After the students leave for the day, Mrs. Brisbane comes over to our table by the window. She is humming happily.

"I guess you fellows are wondering what you'll be doing when school is over," she says with a grin.

Humphrey lets out another series of SQUEAK-SQUEAK-SQUEAKs, and Mrs. Brisbane explains that it's a surprise.

Surprises like a tasty mosquito who flies right into my mouth are nice. But I don't like surprises like hungry snapping turtles with huge jaws. Especially Chopper, who also lived in the swamp with me.

I don't think Humphrey likes surprises of *any* kind.

Once we're alone, my neighbor is quiet until it gets dark and Aldo comes in to clean Room 26, as he does on every weeknight.

He's extra cheery as he goes to work. He tells us that school is already over for him, and he got good grades.

Aldo is bigger and older than the big tads, but he still goes to school to learn to be a teacher like Mrs. Brisbane.

Tonight, he cleans the room as he's never cleaned it before. He whistles, twirls his broom and practically dances across the floor. When he settles down to eat his sandwich, he tells us, "When Longfellow School closes next week, I'm leaving town!"

Aldo seems pleased about leaving, but I see Humphrey's tail twitch and his whiskers droop.

When we're alone again, Humphrey crawls into his little sleeping hut, and I don't see him again the rest of the night. Poor guy. He loves school so much, and now so do I.

It's time to float in the water and let my thoughts wander.

I can almost hear Uncle Chinwag back in the swamp, saying, "Float. Doze. *Be.* And you will live so happily."

But I'm not feeling so hoppy tonight, so I dive into the water side of my tank and splash around until I am as tired as a hummingbird flying against a heavy wind.

Then I hop back up on my rock and go to sleep.

🐾 🐾 🐾 🐾

When our principal, Mr. Morales, visits our classroom, he seems as happy about the end of school as Aldo and Mrs. Brisbane are. He and his family are going to "hit the road," he says. I think it means they are leaving town, too.

Mrs. Brisbane explains that she and her husband are going to Tokyo, where their son is getting married. That's a long way from here. Are Humphrey and I going, too? Is that the surprise?

"*SQUEAK-SQUEAK-SQUEAK!*" By now, I know those are squeaks of alarm.

Our future is as mysterious as the Great Unknown, as we called the world beyond the swamp.

Over the next few days, the students in Room 26 are as busy and buzzy as bees in a field of flowers. There are reports to be graded, desks to be cleaned out and books to return to the library.

But why does school have to end? And where will that leave Humphrey and me?

🐾 🐾 🐾 🐾

Speaking of Humphrey, I don't know what in the swamp he's thinking, but I do know his busy brain is always working.

Once we're alone that night, the little fellow jiggles his lock and scampers over to my tank.

"SQUEAK-SQUEAK-SQUEAK! SQUEAK-SQUEAK-*SQUEAK*!"

Then he scrambles to the edge of the table and slides down the leg, as fast as an eagle swooping down on a lizard. That's *fast*.

Still moving quickly, he hurries across the floor, then flattens himself so he can slide under the door and out into the hallway.

"Be careful, Humphrey!" I try to warn him. But it's too late. He's gone.

I don't see Humphrey again for a long time.

I should be used to watching him go off on a nighttime adventure. He does it often.

Truthfully, I'm a little jealous. I'm an adventurous guy, too. I'd like to go exploring at night, the way he does. But I can't slide down the table leg, squeeze under the door or let myself dry out.

So, I'm left behind. And every single time, I'm as nervous as a mouse listening to the midnight hoots of an owl until he comes back.

While I wait, I dive into my water and swim laps, wondering what my furry friend could be doing all this time. Where can he be? What is he thinking?

A song drifts into my head, and as I often do, I calm myself by singing.

Humphrey loves to help his friends,
He's a daring class pet,

But he is roaming far away,
And he has not come back yet.

Humphrey Hamster, please come home,
Humphrey Hamster, hurry!
If you are not back here soon,
I will turn gray with worry!

My tank isn't big, so I swim a *lot* of laps before Humphrey finally crawls under the door again.

"BOING-BOING!" I welcome him. But he still has hard work ahead of him.

Since Humphrey can't slide *up* the table leg, he grabs onto the blinds' cord and swings back and forth, higher and higher, until he's level with the table. Then he lets go and leaps onto the tabletop. Now, *that's* something I'm good at: leaping.

"Welcome back!" I greet him again.

Humphrey doesn't answer. I can tell he's really tired by the way his tail is dragging.

However, he's not too tired to take out the tiny notebook hidden behind the mirror in his cage and scratch away with his little pencil.

Scritch-scritch-scritch!

Poor guy. I wish he could chill out.

I float in the water again, trying to relax, but I keep wondering: Where did my pal go tonight?

On the last day, it seems as if one minute Mrs. Brisbane is taking attendance, and the next thing I know, she's checking to see that the big tads have emptied their desks.

Late in the day, the door opens and someone unexpected enters. I know her, of course. I remember her bouncy dark curls and her smiling face.

The big tads cheer loudly when she arrives, but Humphrey is unusually silent. That surprises me, because the one thing I know about Ms. Mac is that she and Humphrey are special friends.

In fact, I think he loves her.

"Am I too early?" Ms. Mac asks.

Mrs. Brisbane says her timing is perfect.

Then Ms. Mac speaks to the big tads about their summer plans, which is nice.

But the next words she says change everything.

"I just want you to know that your friends Humphrey and Og are going to have a fantastic summer, too. Because they are coming with *me!*"

I don't know where Ms. Mac is taking us, but at least I know someone will be looking out for us, and I whoop out, "BOING-BOING-BOING-BOING-BOING!"

Ms. Mac laughs and then says something that makes my heart leap. "We are going to have a *great* adventure!" she announces.

Before I know it, the bell rings and the big tads rush out, with Garth in the lead, as always.

Humphrey squeaks a farewell, and he's still squeaking as I take a deep dive off my rock. It's cooling and calming in the water, so I can think about what just happened: the end of school.

Then I remember Granny Greenleaf saying, "If you think more about where you've been than about where you're going, you'll never get anywhere."

At least Humphrey and I are going *somewhere*, and we're going there with Ms. Mac.

I like her a lot. When she comes into the room, she's like a breath of fresh air. Besides the fact that Ms. Mac is nice, all I know about her is that long before I came to school, she was substituting for Mrs. Brisbane. She's the human who went to the pet shop and brought Humphrey back to Room 26.

She picked him out . . . and that's why they have a special friendship.

It was a good decision to make Humphrey a classroom pet.

But then a funny little thought hops into my head: Ms. Mac has known Humphrey a lot longer than she's known me. She knows *he'll* have a wonderful summer. But what about me?

The first thing I learn about Ms. Mac is that she doesn't waste time. She says good-bye to Mrs. Brisbane, and in a flash, we're on our way.

I'm not sure where we're going, but at the rate Ms. Mac is moving, we'll get there quickly. She's as peppy as a frog who swallowed some bees. Believe me, nothing can get you hopping like swallowing a couple of buzzing bees.

Ms. Mac lives in an apartment, which means there are different homes grouped together in one building. Her apartment is full of nice bright light and colorful pictures on the wall.

"Welcome back, Humphrey!" Ms. Mac places his cage on a big round table. "You remember living here before?"

Humphrey answers with a happy squeak.

So, he lived here before? I always thought Ms. Mac brought him directly from the pet shop to school. They know each other even better than I thought.

Once we're settled, Ms. Mac checks Humphrey's cage to make sure everything is in its right place. "There, Humphrey. Your mirror and hamster wheel are right where you like them," she says. "And you have nice clean water."

"SQUEAK-SQUEAK-*SQUEAK*!" he thanks her.

Ms. Mac inspects my tank next. "Hmm," she says. "I'm not sure exactly where things go, Og. And I have a little trouble understanding you. But I'll learn."

"BOING-*BOING*!" I answer.

She chuckles. "No wonder the children say you're funny!"

"I'm not trying to be funny," I respond. "I'm trying to talk!"

This time, she starts to laugh, then she stops herself and leans toward my tank. "I'm sorry, Og. I'm not laughing at you. I think you have a fabulous voice," she says.

"You should hear me sing," I tell her.

She smiles at my boings, but she doesn't laugh again. "I don't know much about frogs," she tells me. "But I have a book, so I can figure out exactly what you need."

She holds it up. It's a big thick book. I hope she's a fast reader, because I'm a little hungry.

Luckily, the food section is near the front of the book, and I get some tasty mealworms for dinner. Not as nice as a juicy cricket, but least I'm not hungry anymore.

❦ ❦ ❦ ❦

The days at Ms. Mac's are quiet, except for the music that is almost always playing in the background.

Some nights, Ms. Mac makes a maze on the floor and lets Humphrey out of his cage. He is good at running through mazes, especially if there are a few sunflower seeds at the end.

"I'd take you out, Og, but I'm not sure if you should be out of the water," she tells me.

I think she needs to read faster.

One day, she does a thorough tank clean, following the book step by step, and she cleans Humphrey's cage as well.

At least I'm in good hands, but I'm not sure I'll ever be as close to Ms. Mac as Humphrey is.

So far, it's a good summer, although I don't see it as the great adventure Ms. Mac mentioned the day she took us home.

A nice, cozy break, yes. A great adventure, no.

Then one evening, the music gets turned up and the doorbell starts ringing. Before I know it, Ms. Mac is introducing us to a parade of friends, many of them carrying dishes and bowls full of food.

"Dion, Annie, Marcus—meet Humphrey and Og!" She brings them over to our table.

"Oooh, what a fine-looking frog," the woman called Annie says. "And the hamster is adorable!" she adds.

We meet even more friends. Andre, Evelyn, Joe. They all linger around the table to "ooh" and "ahh" over Humphrey and me.

"SQUEAK!" my neighbor greets them.

"BOING-BOING!" I add.

The man called Andre says, "That was original!"

"Thank you," I boing.

I have spent many boisterous evenings in the swamp with the sounds of howling, chirping and hooting. But this evening at Ms. Mac's is every bit as noisy as that—without the annoying RUM-RUMMINGs of the bullying bullfrogs.

As the music goes on, the dancing begins. More people come through the door. Vic from next door and Maura from downstairs arrive and, well, I lose count of all the guests.

And then I hear it. BEAT-BEAT-BEAT. BONGA-BONGA-BONG!

Ms. Mac is bringing out some drums—a pair of them—and pounding out a beat.

"How do you like these bongo drums, Og?" she asks.

"Bongo?" I ask. My whole head vibrates at the sound of that word, because Bongo was my name back in the swamp! But Ms. Mac doesn't know that.

BONGA-BONGA-BONG! she plays.

I can't help but join in. "BING-BANG-BOING!" I twang.

The crowd loves it.

"Go, Og!" someone cries.

Ms. Mac plays a little louder and a little faster.

"BING-BANG-*BOING*!" I repeat.

The crowd cheers. I think I hear some piercing SQUEAKs in the background.

I start hopping to the beat of the drum. The sound reminds me so much of warm summer nights in the swamp, when all the creatures are at their noisiest.

The background music is the constant chirping of the crickets and the loud, deep voices of the bullfrogs going, "RUM-RUM-RUM-RUM!" Owl hoots and the high-pitched "kee-aahs" of hawks add to the night music, along with the beat of the woodpecker drumming away at a nearby tree. RAT-A-TAT-A-TAT!

Once, a chorus of green frogs even sang a song about me! My heart swelled with pride.

I don't usually sing in front of humans, but I can't help myself.

> There was a swamp where lived a frog
> And Bongo was his name-o.
> B-O-N-G-O!
> B-O-N-G-O!
> B-O-N-G-O!
> And Bongo was his name-o.

Everyone's dancing now, except Ms. Mac, who is pounding those drums.

I glance over at Humphrey's cage. He's hanging from the top bars of his cage, squeaking his lungs out. "SQUEAK-SQUEAK-SQUEAK-A! SQUEAK-SQUEAK-SQUEAK-A!"

"More, Og, more!" the humans shout.

So, I give them more.

> And in a classroom lived that frog
> And Bongo was his name-o.
> B-O-N-G-O!
> B-O-N-G-O!
> B-O-N-G-O!
> And Bongo was his name-o.

The sound was deafening, but the neighbors didn't care because they were all at the party, too!

The festivities keep going for a long time. And when the music stops, Humphrey is nowhere to be found.

"Humphrey, where are you?" Ms. Mac scurries around the apartment looking for him.

I hear a weak squeak, and when she checks his cage, she spots him in his sleeping hut.

"Sleep well," Ms. Mac whispers to him.

She comes over to my tank and flashes a big smile. Nobody smiles quite like Ms. Mac. "You were certainly the life of the party, Og," she says.

"You weren't so bad yourself," I reply.

"You'd better get some sleep, Mr. BING-BANG-BOING, like your friend Humphrey, because we've got a big trip coming up," she says.

"Where are we going?" I ask.

"For some folks, vacations mean relaxing and doing nothing," she explains. "But me? I like an adventurous vacation where I see new things and meet new people. And animals," she says. "I have a feeling you do, too."

"Animals? What animals will we be meeting?" I ask.

She turns off the light and leaves the room before I get an answer. And she expects me to sleep tonight?

I cool off in the water for a while. I'm not sure if I am asleep or awake because the whole evening has seemed like one big, noisy, wonderful dream.

Road Trip

· · · · · · · · · · · · · · · ·

At the end of the stream there's
always a new beginning.
—Granny Greenleaf's
Wildlife Wisdom

I watch every move Ms. Mac makes the next day. She washes and sews, sorts and folds clothes, always humming a happy tune. I wish she'd get those bongo drums out again.

She pulls a suitcase out of the closet and then . . . she leaves!

Humphrey and I don't say much. We sit and wait, but nothing happens.

This is our great adventure?

Humphrey dozes off, and I hum a new verse to the song from last night.

There was a frog who got so bored
And Bongo was his name-o.

Yawn, yawn, yawn, yawn, yawn!
Yawn—

The door swings open, and Ms. Mac hurries in, her arms loaded with shopping bags. "Sorry I was gone so long," she says. "I had a lot to get, including more food for you two."

"Squeak!" Humphrey says.

"We won't be near a town," she explains. "I bet you guys will be as happy to get out in nature as I will."

BING-BANG-BOING! We *are* going somewhere wild. "Out in nature," she just said.

"SQUEAK-SQUEAK-*SQUEAK*!" my excited neighbor exclaims.

"The call of the wild must be answered," she adds with a grin.

I dive into the water and start swimming laps.

I grew up in the wild, and I'm going back to the wild tomorrow. Will there be a swamp? Will there be *my* swamp? Will there be lots of yummy crickets, mosquitoes, beetles and dragonflies? Will there be—

Screech-screech-screech!

I glance over at Humphrey, who is spinning on his wheel like crazy. I wish someone could fix that screech.

Until now, I haven't thought about his summer. He may not like being out in the wild. He might not like mosquitoes or dragonflies, not to mention bats, snakes and bullying bullfrogs.

Ms. Mac leans down by my tank. "Og, you know every-thing about living in the wild," she tells me. "But Humphrey . . ."

She looks over at his cage. He's spinning his wheel so fast, he's just a blur.

"He doesn't know anything outside the human world," she says.

Ms. Mac is right. I was so excited about being back out-side, I'd forgotten that Humphrey has always lived inside.

"I hope you'll look out for him," she continues.

You bet I will! "BOING-BOING! BOING-BOING!" I assure her. "I promise!"

ᘺ ᘺ ᘺ ᘺ

Riding in a car isn't comfortable for me, and this ride is so bumpy, huge waves are breaking in my tank water. If only I had a surfboard!

I try to sit on my rock but keep sliding off, so I just float and hope the road smooths out soon.

It's certainly a rough start to our big adventure. And the loud music Ms. Mac is playing makes it even wilder.

Once or twice I boing to Humphrey to ask if he's okay. I hear a few weak squeaks in return.

I'm so busy trying to stay afloat, I don't have much time to think about where we're headed. Maybe that's a good thing, because I have a nagging worry in the back of my mind about the new animals she said we'd be meeting.

Suddenly, Ms. Mac turns off the music and stops the car. "Oh, wow," she says.

The water in my tank is calmer now, and I feel a breeze drifting in through the open door.

But it's not like the breeze that occasionally floats through the window in Room 26. This breeze carries a million trillion smells of grass and mud, trees and flowers, and also a hint of squirrels, foxes, mice, birds and things that Humphrey has probably never smelled before. Me? I've smelled them *all* before.

"You okay, buddy?" I ask Humphrey.

He doesn't answer. Maybe he's hearing the skittering mice outside the car and the human footsteps coming closer.

Then I hear a man's voice. "Well, who do we have here?" it asks.

My heart beats like a bongo drum. That voice reminds me of the man who found me back in McKenzie's Marsh. The voice that said "gotcha" as he captured me and took me away from my friends and family and life as I knew it.

I'm lucky that I ended up in Longfellow School, where there's so much to do that most days I don't have time to miss the swamp, but I don't ever want to run into that human again!

I'm relieved when I finally see the man's smiling face and his bright red hair. He's definitely not the frognapper! In fact, whatever this place is, he owns it.

When he introduces himself, he has a friendly name. "Call me Hap," he says. "And welcome to Happy Hollow."

What I can see from the car looks happy, too. Blue sky, green trees and grass.

Then I hear Hap say that we're spending the night in a robin's nest, and I'm confused. Does he think I'm a tree frog? (I am not.) And if Ms. Mac is with us, how will the three of us fit?

"We're still getting the counselors' cabins fixed up, but the kids' are ready," he explains.

The Robins' Nest turns out to be a small wooden building with a porch.

"This is a cozy cabin," Ms. Mac says, opening the door.

Inside, I spot a couple of beds stacked on top of each other, but other than that, there's not a lot of furniture—just wooden floors, wooden walls, a wooden ceiling.

There *is* a table by a window, and that's where Ms. Mac sets my tank and Humphrey's cage. And then she leaves. With all that green grass and blue sky and toadally frog-alicious smells outside, we're stuck *inside*.

So much for the call of the wild!

I dive into the water and take a lazy swim while Humphrey stares out the window.

When I see the little guy jiggle the lock on his cage, I hop back on my rock. What is my adventurous pal going to do? "What's up, buddy?" I boing.

I'm half expecting him to slide down the table leg, the

way he does in Room 26, but Humphrey is unpredictable, as always.

He scampers up the *outside* of his cage, all the way to the top, and looks out the window.

(He may be furry, but he's as nimble as a lizard.)

Humphrey spends a long time staring out the window and listening to the sounds. He must hear what I hear: laughter and singing off in the distance, some hammering and clanking. And later, the far-off sounds of bongo drums.

Once the sun is low in the sky, I worry that Ms. Mac will come back and find Humphrey outside of his cage. If that ever happens, some human will probably fix that lock, and Humphrey's secret escape route—which only I know about—will be closed forever.

I don't think he wants to be trapped any more than I do, and I'm relieved when he crawls back in his cage and closes the door behind him.

Ms. Mac comes in late and gets up early. The time in between seems awfully long with me stuck in my tank and Humphrey in his cage. Long enough to notice *the sound*.

It's a scritchy, scratchy noise. From my time in the swamp, I'd guess it was coming from a mouse or a rat or something a lot larger.

Whoever is making that sound has a lot of energy, because I hear it all day long and into the night.

I can tell that Humphrey hears it, too. From time to

time, he squeaks at me, but of course, I can't actually understand what he's saying.

I tell him, "I don't know, pal. I just don't know."

The scritching and scratching is clearly getting on Humphrey's nerves, and finally, he swings open the cage door again.

"Where are you going, buddy?" I ask nervously. "Better be careful!"

Luckily, Humphrey quickly pulls the door closed again as Ms. Mac comes back into the cabin.

Whew! A close one!

I'm used to Humphrey taking chances, and I admire his adventurous spirit. But even though the cabin is boring, there is real wildlife right outside, and I'm not sure he knows how dangerous it is. And Ms. Mac did tell me to look out for the furry fellow.

Now she tells us, "Things are about to start popping," which sounds interesting. Then she picks up Humphrey's cage and leaves the cabin.

I panic a little. For one thing, I don't know where she's taking him.

Wherever it is, I don't want to be left behind.

But she comes back for my tank a few minutes later and carries it through the woods, past other cabins that look like the Robins' Nest. I see blue sky and green trees and grass and smell aromas I'd almost forgotten!

It's a lot like home. I mean my *first* home.

At the end of the trail is a big wooden building with a sign outside that says HAPPY HOLLOW HALL. The path down is very bumpy, and there's a tidal wave in my tank. I feel like a mosquito caught in a hurricane.

When we get inside, I can hear voices and squeaking, but I'm not sure what anyone is saying. I just try to keep my head above water.

We pass through a large room full of tables and chairs that looks a lot like Ms. Mac's living room but bigger.

Once the waves calm down, I see that my tank is next to Humphrey's cage and we're facing another window. It's nice to look out at the trees and grass, but it would be even nicer to *be* outside.

Humphrey's squeaks suddenly sound excited.

And then I hear it: "Never fear 'cause Aldo's here!"

I can't believe my eyes. Aldo is standing right next to us! He tells us he's going to be at camp, too, as a counselor. I'm not sure what a counselor is, but it sounds like someone helpful and wise, like old Uncle Chinwag back in the swamp.

"That's good news!" I boing to him.

And then he introduces his wife, Maria, and explains that she's taking a break from the bakery to cook here for the summer. He adds that it will be the best camp food ever, but can it taste as good as those crickets in the woods?

Maria has warm eyes and a big smile. "At last we meet, Og," she says. "Aldo talks about you all the time!"

Ms. Mac is a counselor, too, and there are others. One of them is called Katie, and she doesn't look much older than the big tads in Room 26. When she leans in to get a closer look at me, she says, "Og, I want a dress that matches your beautiful green skin." I think I'm going to like her!

Hap Holloway welcomes everyone, and there's lots of laughing going on until we hear a familiar voice. It's Mrs. Wright, who teaches physical education at Longfellow School. I don't think she's a big fan of classroom pets like me. And the shrill whistle she wears around her neck makes an earsplitting racket. She uses it all the time.

That evening, the counselors all eat pizza and sing. Ms. Mac plays the bongos, and Katie plays a guitar. Those twangy strings sound a lot like me.

Between the BONG-BONGs of the drums and the BOING-BOING of the guitar, I feel right at home!

$$\text{✿ ✿ ✿ ✿}$$

The next day, Humphrey and I are still by the window in the rec room when cars start pulling up outside.

"Let the fun begin!" Ms. Mac says. "Camp is officially in session!" She hurries outside to greet the new arrivals.

I expect to see more counselors, but instead, I am amazed to see whole families getting out of the cars, carrying all kinds of suitcases and backpacks.

I'm even more amazed to see humans I know from Room 26! Richie and Gail are there, and a smaller boy that might be Gail's brother. Here comes Sayeh and—wait—it's Miranda! She's with another girl her age. Whose loud voice is that? It's A.J., of course, with his younger brother, Ty, and his best friend, Garth.

They're all as excited to see me and Humphrey as we are to see them.

Of course, there are lots of big tads I don't know at all. I will be meeting a lot of new humans.

Then something unexpected happens. The parents all leave their children behind and drive away!

☙ ☙ ☙ ☙

Camp Happy Hollow is a surprising place. But Ms. Mac said it would be an adventure, and I'm ready for that! So, while Humphrey naps that afternoon, a new song to celebrate the start of camp pops into my head.

A-camping we will go,
A-camping we will go,
Hi-ho the derry-o,
A-camping we will go.

With friends tried and true,
And friends that are new,
Hi-ho the derry-o,
A-camping we will go.

With lots of fresh air,
And trees everywhere,
Hi-ho the derry-o,
A-camping we will go.

I'm used to the noise of the swamp and the classroom. A few nights ago, I had the time of my life at Ms. Mac's party. BING-BANG-BONGO! It was loud, but I didn't mind. But this first night at camp makes me wish I had earplugs, even though you can't see my ears. (They're right behind my eyes, and they are covered with a thin layer of skin. But I hear just fine, thank you.)

As everyone gathers in the dining hall, it's full of loud chatter and shrieks of laughter. There's singing and noisy forks and knives and an occasional shrill blast from Mrs. Wright's whistle.

Ms. Mac was right about one thing: This place is *wild*.

When Hap introduces Humphrey and me, the cheering is deafening, but it is certainly a warm welcome.

Then comes the BIG news—to me at least. Humphrey and I will be staying in different cabins each night, but we won't be together. We're a reward to the cabins for obeying the rules.

After dinner, the campers are sent outside for a campfire. Most creatures run away from fires, but everyone at Happy Hollow runs *toward* a fire. I don't mind skipping that.

Then it's quiet again, except for distant singing, until A.J. rushes in and takes Humphrey's cage. "You get to stay with the Blue Jays tonight!" he says.

Miranda grabs my tank and says I am going to the Robins' Nest.

"Good luck!" I tell Humphrey as A.J. races out of sight.

"SQUEAK!" he replies.

And I don't see him again until morning.

Learning the Ropes

· · · · · · · · · · · · · · · ·

Listening is learning.

—Granny Greenleaf's
Wildlife Wisdom

The Robins' Nest has changed since last night. Now it is full of girls. And me, of course.

"Og, I'm so happy you're here," Miranda tells me.

"Me too!" I say truthfully.

The girls all unpack and get ready for bed, except for Gail, who just sits on the edge of her bed, frowning at the floor.

I am confused because back in Room 26, Gail is always giggling. I haven't even seen her *smile* since she arrived at camp.

"Isn't it great to see Og again?" Miranda asks her.

Gail doesn't look up. "Sure," she says.

She doesn't sound like she means it, but I don't take it personally.

Then Gail blows out a huge sigh. "I wish *all* my friends were here," she adds.

Miranda looks puzzled. "*I'm* your friend."

"I know," Gail answers. She still doesn't smile.

A girl called Lindsey, who's making the bed above Gail's, says, "I don't know anyone here, but it seems like a fun place."

Gail still hangs her head. I want to be encouraging, so I chime in. "BOING-BOING!"

Lindsey leaps up off her bed. "What was *that*?"

"That noise?" Miranda points at me. "It's Og."

"No way." A camper named Kayla laughs. "Frogs croak or say 'ribbit.'"

"Og's a special frog," Miranda tells her. "Right, Gail?"

Gail glumly nods.

"Thank you!" I answer.

"He did it again!" Lindsey tries to imitate my twangy voice. "BOING-BOING!"

Kayla joins in. "BOING-BOING-BOING-BOING!"

Miranda laughs, too. "I guess we're used to it. Right, Gail?"

This time Gail barely nods.

Kneeling next to my tank, Lindsey stares at me. "He's the cutest thing I've ever seen."

Me? Cute? Awwww. I'll bet the crickets back in the swamp didn't think I was so cute!

"Let's take him out and play with him." Lindsey slides the top off my tank.

"No!" Miranda jumps up. "He doesn't like to be handled."

"I'll be careful," Lindsey says.

Miranda shakes her head. "No. It's not a good idea."

Thank goodness Miranda knows me so well. I really do *not* like to be handled.

Lindsey grudgingly slides the top back in place and bends down so her nose is almost touching my tank.

"Say hi again, Og!"

"Hello!" I answer.

She dissolves into giggles. A funny thing I've noticed about humans: Once one of them starts to giggle, people around them giggle, too. While Miranda and Kayla laugh loudly, the giggliest girl from Room 26 remains gloomy.

The rest of the girls are still laughing at my boings when Ms. Mac comes in to check on us. "What's so funny?" she asks.

"Og!" Lindsey points to my tank. "He's sooo cute!"

"That's our Og," Ms. Mac says. So she thinks I'm cute, too!

"How's camp going so far?" she asks.

Miranda smiles and answers, "Great!"

Lindsey and a few other girls give Ms. Mac the thumbs-up sign. I wish I could do that!

Kayla says, "This place is cool."

Only one girl doesn't say anything.

"Gail?" Ms. Mac goes over to her bed. "Are you okay?"

Still hanging her head, Gail mumbles, "Yeah."

Ms. Mac pats Gail on the back and sends the other girls out to get washed up.

Once they're gone, Ms. Mac sits next to Gail on the bed. "What's wrong?"

"I don't like camp," Gail answers.

Ms. Mac asks her if it's the food, and Gail shrugs. Ms. Mac asks her if she isn't getting along with the other campers. Gail shrugs again.

"Look, you just got here," Ms. Mac says. "You haven't given it a chance yet, right?"

"Mm-hmm," Gail replies.

"So, will you promise that tomorrow you'll try to smile and join in? Just *try*. I think everything will look better in the morning."

The other girls return, and Gail goes out to brush her teeth.

When she's gone, Miranda tells Ms. Mac that the problem is that Gail misses Heidi, her best friend. "They do everything together," Miranda explains.

Ms. Mac nods. "I know. You girls can help by trying to get her more involved."

Kayla says, "She seems stuck-up to me."

Miranda assures her that Gail is usually a lot of fun. "I promise, we'll try to make her feel better," she tells Ms. Mac.

Good old Miranda. She's always willing to help out.

When Gail returns, Ms. Mac turns out the lights, reminding the girls they have a big day tomorrow.

They all give Gail a cheery "good night."

"Night!" I add, and Lindsey giggles.

"Night, Oggie-woggie!"

That's a new one. I like Oggie, but I'm not sure about *Oggie-woggie*.

Once it's finally quiet, I hear someone sniffling a little. It's not hard to figure out who it is.

I float around my tank and think about my early days after I was frognapped from the swamp. I missed my friends so much it hurt, especially Jumpin' Jack.

I felt as lonely as a frog at a toad family reunion. (Toads are nice enough . . . but they're not *frogs*.)

I guess that's how Gail feels.

Even now, I miss my pal Humphrey. I hope he's doing okay in the Blue Jays' cabin. I hope he's not afraid of the wild smells outside or the scratchy sounds under the floor.

The sniffling stops, and it's quiet in the Robins' Nest.

I vow to help Gail feel better in the morning, but it won't be easy peasy.

☙ ☙ ☙ ☙

The girls and I wake up to music so loud, I think it would drown out the bullying bullfrogs. That's *loud*!

Ms. Mac pops her head in the door. "Rise and shine, ladies. Breakfast in half an hour. Be there or be square!"

There are some groans as the girls get up. They are definitely not shining.

"How'd you sleep, Gail?" Miranda asks.

"Okay, I guess," Gail answers gloomily.

Maybe she's going to start trying to be more involved *after* breakfast.

After getting dressed, the Robins rush around cleaning the cabin. Gail pitches in, but she still doesn't look happy.

Ms. Mac checks on the girls' progress and then tells them to head down to the dining hall.

"You too, Og," she says, picking up my tank.

Later, Humphrey joins me on the table in the rec room, squeaking nonstop.

"Squeak-squeak-*squeak*!" he repeats over and over.

Maybe he's trying to tell me he missed me.

He seems to want an answer, so I finally boing, "Whatever you say, Humphrey," and he quiets down.

Before we even have time to get settled, Ms. Mac picks up Humphrey's cage, and Katie takes my tank. "Come on. We're putting you to work!" Ms. Mac tells us.

Hey, nobody said anything about us working before. I guess this isn't a vacation after all.

"Squeak-squeak-squeak!" my pal says. Maybe he thought it was a vacation, too.

They carry us to a large cabin with one wall completely

open to the outside. From the front porch, I spot something through the trees that makes my heart beat like a bongo drum. Water! In the distance, there's a pond or a lake or maybe even a swamp! I hope I can get a better look at it soon.

Inside, the cabin reminds me of a classroom with tables and chairs. There's no chalkboard, but there are big charts on the wall. One is all about trees, one is all about leaves, and one shows animal tracks.

BING-BANG-*BOING*! There's even a frog footprint!

"Welcome to the Nature Center," Ms. Mac says as Katie sets my tank on a table next to Humphrey's cage.

But Humphrey and I are not alone. Farther down the table is a shifty-eyed character Katie calls Jake.

I hop up on my rock to get a better look, and Humphrey scampers to the top of his cage.

When he sees Jake, he squeaks in alarm, and I totally understand.

Jake, it turns out, is a snake.

Humphrey probably never saw one before, but I have had a lot of experiences with snakes—all unpleasant! Now, not *all* snakes are bad, but I'd never turn my back on one. At an early age, Granny Greenleaf taught us young tads that "if you see a snake, you should worry . . . and hop away in a great big hurry."

A few tads who didn't take her advice were sorry later!

There's another creature on the table, one that's a bit less scary than a snake.

"This is Lovey Dovey. She's a mourning dove we found in the woods with a broken wing," Ms. Mac explains. "She's almost healed now."

Mourning doves have a low, sad call, which Lovey demonstrates. "Woo-oo-oo-oo."

"Eeek!" Humphrey exclaims. I guess he never heard a dove before.

When Ms. Mac explains that the campers will be coming in for nature classes, Humphrey leaps on his wheel and spins. If you can believe it, he starts going even faster when the kids arrive.

I think he likes being a classroom pet again. I do, too, but I am keeping my eye on Jake.

Katie gives an interesting talk about animal tracks and then passes out sheets of paper to the campers.

"See if you can match the track to the animal," she explains. "Just draw a line from each set of tracks to the animal you think makes those tracks."

"Do we get graded?" A.J. asks.

Katie smiles. "No, it's just for fun."

I'm pretty sure if I took the test, I'd get them all right. But these big tads have never lived in the swamp, like I did!

While they're working, Katie lets them take turns coming over to see Humphrey and me and sketching our feet. Or in Humphrey's case, his paws.

I sit on my rock so they can get a good look at mine.

"Please hold still, Humphrey," Sayeh tells my neighbor. "If you don't, my drawing will look all blurry."

He tries, but it's not easy for a hamster to sit still for long.

Then Katie tells the class the answers to the worksheet.

"Yes!" Noah looks pleased with himself. "I knew I'd get them all right."

I can see that Noah knows a lot, but he reminds me a little of the bullying bullfrogs back in the swamp. According to them, they were the smartest, loudest, bravest, fastest animals in the swamp.

Well, they *were* the loudest.

At the end of the session, Ms. Mac asks Miranda if she can stay for a minute.

"Squeak!" Humphrey says in alarm.

I'm surprised, too, because I didn't see Miranda do anything wrong, and at school, if you're asked to stay after class, it's because there's a problem.

When the rest of the campers are gone, Ms. Mac tells Miranda that she got a call from her mom.

"Oh," Miranda says.

"She wants to make sure I am following the list she sent us," Ms. Mac continues. "Do you know about the list?"

Miranda nods.

Ms. Mac takes a piece of paper out of her pocket and reads: " 'Dos and Don'ts for Miranda. No horseback riding, make sure she has a blanket at night because she gets cold easily, please check to see that she always has a water bottle with her, please allow her to make a short call to me each evening, let me know immediately if she has to see the nurse . . .' That's a lot of rules."

Miranda sighs. "I know. She worries."

"That is completely understandable. I assured her that the counselors are all trained, and we do the worrying here so the parents don't have to. Do you *want* to go horseback riding?" Ms. Mac asks.

"I'd like to try it," Miranda says. "But I promised Mom I wouldn't. She thinks I'm too small."

"You aren't particularly small for your age," Ms. Mac says. "We have different sizes of horses."

"I know," Miranda answers. "She just doesn't want me to." She hesitates. "My mom didn't even want me to go to camp, but my dad did. They're divorced."

Ms. Mac nods.

"She finally said yes, but then she wished she hadn't," Miranda explains.

"Aren't you related to Abby?" Ms. Mac asks. "She signed up for horseback riding."

Miranda nods. "She's my stepsister. And my best friend. But we have different moms."

"Okay," Ms. Mac says. "Most campers alternate horseback riding and swimming every other day. So, do you want to go swimming every day?"

"I guess," Miranda answers.

I may not understand humans completely, but I think she *really* wants to go horseback riding.

"We've had a few campers who are allergic to horses and don't ride," Ms. Mac says. "But the next thing on the list says, 'No swimming if the water is cold.'"

"The water won't be cold now, will it?" Miranda asks.

Ms. Mac thinks about it for a second. "No, but it can be a little *brisk*."

"Oh," Miranda says.

"Miranda, I don't want you to disobey your mom, but she knew when she signed you up for camp that there would be no phone calls, only letters. Are you enjoying camp?"

Miranda's face lights up. "I love it! Everybody's so nice."

"I told her she can check our website for news and photos every day. But when you write your mom today, why don't you let her know that you're having fun. Tell her some of the good things about camp, and maybe she won't be so anxious," Ms. Mac suggests.

Miranda agrees, but she looks down when she leaves.

Once we're alone, Humphrey scampers to the side of his cage nearest me. "SQUEAK-SQUEAK-SQUEAK? SQUEAK-SQUEAK-SQUEAK!"

"I know," I tell him. "I'm a little confused, too."

The Thing in the Woods

· · · · · · · · · · · · · · · · ·

The scariest creature is the one
you've never seen.

—Granny Greenleaf's
Wildlife Wisdom

Moving from cabin to cabin each night is interesting, but it can be confusing. I have a new appreciation for what Humphrey's life is like, spending each weekend with a different family. I'm used to quiet weekends, mostly in Room 26, except for an occasional visit to a house. But I'm ready to mix it up this summer!

The second night, it's my turn to stay with the Bobwhites.

"If our cabin is going to be named after a bird, why can't it be something cool, like an eagle or a falcon?" Garth complains as the campers gather in the cabin after the evening campfire.

Ty, who is A.J.'s younger brother, says, "Who is Bob White anyway?"

"Don't you know anything?" Noah asks. I'm afraid he's not going to be popular if he keeps talking like that.

"I know plenty," Ty mutters as Noah continues.

"A bobwhite is a quail that makes a strange sound," he says. "People think it sounds like 'Bob White.' Like this."

Noah clears his throat before imitating the bird. "Bob-*white*! Bob-*white*! Hear how my voice goes up with the second part?"

Some of the other boys try it. "Bob-*white*! Bob-*white*!"

Then they burst out laughing.

"That is pretty cool," a boy called Sam replies. "That could be our cabin's special call."

They stop laughing when suddenly a different bird in the woods calls out, "Whoo! Whoo!"

Of course, everybody knows what *that* is.

I shiver as I remember how owls love to hunt mice at night. And mice are a lot like—I hate to say it—hamsters. I hope Humphrey doesn't jiggle open his lock tonight!

"That's nothing compared to the sound the Howler makes," Garth says. "Hap Holloway said it's blood-curling."

What? Blood that curls? A Howler? I have no idea what he's talking about.

"Owoooo," the boys all howl.

"I'd sure like to win the Clash of the Cabins so we can go to Haunted Hollow and see the Howler for ourselves," Sam says. "It sounds like something from a scary movie."

"Yeah," Garth agrees. "A ferocious beast covered with

fur, with huge sharp fangs, big feet and a bad smell. Oh, and a loud voice!"

"Owoooo," he and Sam repeat.

Ty looks worried. "I'm not sure I want to see him."

"Don't worry. The camp wouldn't let anything bad happen to us," Sam tells him. "Our parents would be upset."

I'm not sure that makes Ty feel better. Maybe I don't, either.

I heard part of what Hap Holloway said about the Clash of the Cabins. The campers in each cabin will compete against the other campers in different events—everything from softball, volleyball, swimming and canoeing to trail marking and knot tying. The prize for the winning group is a nighttime visit to a spot called Haunted Hollow, where that scary Howler creature lives.

"I want to win," Garth says. "But I'm not sure we can. A.J. is good at everything, so the Blue Jays will probably win." He should know. A.J. is his best friend.

"Yeah, but Sam is a good athlete, too," Ty reminds him.

"We have plenty of guys who are good at things," Sam says. "If we all give it our best, we have a good chance of seeing the Howler."

"Guys, there's no such thing as a Howler," Noah says. "I've read about every kind of creature on earth, and I never heard of a Howler."

Ty looks worried. "But there still could be one."

My mind races. I know a lot of creatures in the wild, and some of them howl. Wolves. Coyotes. Red-tailed hawks. Some owls and foxes.

They are all chilling, but would they make my blood curl?

"I'll bet the Howler is like those scary creatures that you read about," Garth says. "Like the abdominal snowman."

Noah shakes his head. "It's the *abominable snowman*."

Now I'm wondering if there's an abominable abdominal snowman in Haunted Hollow as well as the Howler.

"It's scary whatever you call it," Ty says. "I bet the first person who heard the Howler invented the word 'blood-curdling.'"

Oh. So it's not *curling*, but it's still frightening.

The conversation is interrupted when Aldo comes in to tell the boys to get ready for bed.

"Aldo?" Garth asks. "Have you seen the Howler?"

"Well . . ." Aldo pauses. "I can't really talk about it."

"Where is this Haunted Hollow? Can we see it from camp?" Ty asks.

Aldo grins. "You guys sure have a lot of questions. You can't see it from camp. It's in the dense woods down there on the other side of the lake. If you want to see it, you'll have to work hard to win the Clash of the Cabins! So, you guys think you have a chance?"

"Absolutely!" Sam says.

"But you're good at sports," Garth tells Sam. "I'm not."

"You all have strengths. *I* think you can do it." Aldo points to his head. "Besides, what's up *here* is as important as your talent. As they say, 'Believe it, and you'll achieve it.' Now, time to hustle and get to bed."

Once the lights are out, it takes the Bobwhites a while to get to sleep, and then it gets quiet, except for that owl hooting out in the woods.

As I float in my tank in the darkened cabin, I wonder what Humphrey is doing.

I've heard scary creatures howling in the woods before, but the scariest thing Humphrey has ever heard is Mrs. Wright and her whistle. (She can be frightening, all right.)

But unlike Humphrey and the Bobwhites, I have felt true fear, deep in the night where unseen dangers lurk. And I have an idea that the Howler's scariness is on a whole different level. As I try to imagine what that creature might be like, a song drifts into my head.

What's a Howler?
What's a Howler?
I don't know.
I don't know.
I don't want him to meet me!
I don't want him to eat me!
Stay away.
Stay away.

Throughout the night, I hear a few howls far-off in the woods, but luckily, I recognize them all from my days back in the swamp.

Still, it's a long night.

 ψ ψ ψ ψ

I don't have a lot of time to think about the Howler, because we're so busy. No time to lounge around on a lily pad, the way I did back in the swamp.

Sometimes Humphrey and I get time to rest in the recreation room. He naps in his sleeping hut a lot more often than he did at Longfellow School, and I think about how life in the wild might be a little too much for my furry pal.

From my viewpoint by the window, some other things worry me, too.

I see campers ride by on horses . . . and notice the sad look on Miranda's face as they pass by her.

Then there's Gail, sitting against a tree and writing what is probably another letter to Heidi.

I'm startled when Lindsey suddenly appears outside, standing in front of the window and waving. "Hi, Oggie! You are adorable!"

So I'm not just cute. I am also adorable. That's nice to hear.

She bends closer. "I just want to give you a great big hug!"

That's not nice to hear. I don't like to be squeezed. "Please don't," I boing.

Luckily, a voice on the loudspeaker announces that session three begins in five minutes. Lindsey says, "Bye," and rushes off with the other campers.

I decide to Float. Doze. *Be.* And try not to think about Lindsey hugging me, the problems of my fellow campers or what the Howler is like.

I guess I sleep a bit, because the next thing I know, I'm whisked off to the Chickadees' cabin for the first time. I don't even have a chance to say "Nighty-night" to Humphrey, who is headed to stay with the Bobwhites.

🐾 🐾 🐾 🐾

As always, visiting a new cabin means I meet new campers. The Chickadees are an interesting group. One is the girl who came to camp with Miranda. Her name is Abby, and I remember hearing Miranda tell Ms. Mac she is her stepsister. Which is pretty much like a sister.

Sayeh is also a Chickadee, and I know her well from Room 26. The others, like Val and Marissa, are new to me. I'm always glad to meet new humans.

They come in after the campfire, smelling a little bit smoky. There's an easy, relaxed mood here, which is a far cry from life in the swamp.

Marissa braids Val's hair, while Abby and Sayeh play an interesting game where they chant and clap each other's hands. I like the one about Miss Susie. I wonder if there's a chant about Ms. Mac.

After a while, Abby yawns, then Sayeh. Pretty soon, all the girls are yawning. I've noticed that yawning is like giggling with humans. It seems to be contagious!

ψ ψ ψ ψ

I am well rested when I'm returned to the Nature Center in the morning. My pal's excited squeaks let me know that he's glad to see me.

Sayeh stops by on her way to her desk. As usual, she's as sweet as honeysuckle in summer. Believe me, there's nothing sweeter than honeysuckle.

Her voice is sweet, too, as she sings a song about Camp Happy Hollow to Humphrey.

It's such a good song, I wish I'd written it.

My favorite part is *"for all the days and weeks and years that follow, we'll remember happy days at Happy Hollow."* It makes me feel warm inside.

But that feeling doesn't last when a voice says, "Oooh, hi, Og, you *cutie-wootie!*"

"BOING???"

The voice belongs to Lindsey, of course. Her face is so close to my tank, it looks as big as a full moon.

"I wish I could take you home with me," she says. "You could share my room, and we could do *everything* together. Sleep, eat, have a cuddle!"

Sure, we could share a room, but I'd rather listen to the bullying bullfrogs than be picked up and cuddled! Besides, if a human picks me up and squeezes me, I usually pee. I don't like it, but I can't help it. Humans don't like it, either!

Once class begins, I enjoy hearing Katie talk about wild animal tracks until Noah raises his hand and asks Katie why Humphrey and I are kept in a cage and a tank. *That* gets my attention!

Katie tries to explain, but I don't think Noah is listening.

"I think we should let them out," he says.

Thank goodness Ty speaks up in a voice almost as loud as his brother A.J.'s. "Not if Jake's going to eat Humphrey and Og!"

I glance down the table to check out Jake the Snake. You can never tell what a snake is thinking, but he looks a little hungry to me. I'm pretty sure snakes are *always* hungry . . . especially for frogs.

In fact, I'm not sure about Lovey, either. I never had a problem with doves, but she is a bird, and so are dangerous owls and hawks.

Noah doesn't let up. He keeps insisting that Humphrey and I should be released into the wild.

Quickly, I think of what I'd do if someone let me out. I remember that nice slice of water I saw peeking through the trees, and that's where I'd head. With luck, I'd find some fellow green frogs to help me adjust.

At least I'd know what's in store for me there.

But then I glance over at Humphrey. So small. So furry. So unaware of the dangers out there. No wonder Ms. Mac asked me to look out for him.

She's looking out for both of us now. She explains to Noah that Humphrey and I are classroom pets who are used to being taken care of, and Jake is the camp mascot.

Lovey, on the other hand, is a wild bird who was injured, and I'm hoppy to hear they plan to release her back into the wild soon.

For now, Ms. Mac quiets Noah down.

"Thank you!" I boing.

When I spend the next night with the Blue Jays, I get to see A.J. and Richie from Room 26. There's a boy named Simon who's a little younger. He's the one I saw coming to camp with Gail, so he must be her brother. But the one called Brad gets my attention.

As soon as A.J. sets my tank on a table, Simon and Richie rush over to say hi, but Brad stays on his bed, reading a magazine. He doesn't even look up.

"We won you for the night, Og!" Richie says. "Are you glad?"

"BING-BANG-BOING!" I tell him.

"And how's my favorite classroom frog?" Richie asks.

Brad glances over. *"That's* a classroom pet? A frog?"

"Og is a great pet," A.J. says.

"Frogs can't do anything," Brad complains.

I stick up for frogs everywhere. "BOING-BOING! BOING-BOING!"

"You tell him, Og!" Simon says.

Brad wanders over to the table and looks closer. "All he can do is make that goofy noise. He can't sit or play dead or shake paws like my dog does."

This guy is about as friendly as a water moccasin in a bad mood (which is almost all the time, for a water moccasin).

To show Brad what frogs can do, I take a gigantic leap from my rock, arching high up in the air, then make a beautiful dive into the water. If only Jumpin' Jack could see me now!

Brad shakes his head and returns to his bed. He doesn't look up from his magazine again, not even to talk about the Clash of the Cabins with the rest of the boys.

"Did you see Sam play softball today?" Simon asks. "He hit two home runs and a triple!"

Richie nods. "That's why they call him Super-Sam. I'm not sure how we can beat the Bobwhites with Sam on their side."

"Well, we have to try," A.J. says. "It's at least worth fighting for."

Then the boys (minus Brad) cheer, "Blue Jays rule! Blue

Jays rule!" A.J.'s voice is so loud, I have to swim underwater to muffle the sound.

"Wow, there's some great cabin spirit here!" Aldo says when he comes in. "Keep up the enthusiasm, boys. But now it's time to settle down."

I agree with Aldo about the cabin spirit. But my ears are grateful when the boys stop cheering.

Hoots and Howls

· · · · · · · · · · · · · · · ·

Laughter is nature's best
medicine.

—Granny Greenleaf's
Wildlife Wisdom

D on't ask me how Brad is picked to carry my tank back to
the Nature Center in the morning. Maybe Aldo thinks
he'll be in a better mood if he has something to do.

It's raining a little bit, which doesn't bother me. I love the
feeling of water on my skin, and rain brings mud—my favorite thing!

As he heads down the bumpy path, I'm surprised to hear
Brad talking to me. But it doesn't take long to figure out that
he's actually talking to himself.

"I didn't have to carry a dumb old frog at my old camp,"
he mutters. "Things were fun there."

Okay. I get the idea he doesn't like Camp Happy Hollow,
but he doesn't have to be insulting.

Humphrey is already waiting at the Nature Center. When Brad sets down my tank next to his cage, Brad calls me dumb again and also complains because I don't say *ribbit*.

I have heard frogs chirp, peep, bark, grunt, whistle and croak. Only a few tree frogs say *ribbit*.

Personally, I don't think there's a finer sound than a hearty BOING!

Humphrey squeaks like a whole choir of angry mice. He seems pretty upset about what Brad said to me.

Finally, Brad leaves us alone and ends up sitting next to Gail, who's too busy writing to look up. And I can guess who she's writing to. I hope Heidi has a lot of free time to read all those letters!

Over the past few days, Katie and Ms. Mac have told Gail more than once to stop. The campers are supposed to write letters home in the afternoon. They're *not* supposed to write them all day long.

But Gail is so busy writing her friend back home, I'm not sure she'd recognize her fellow campers' faces. She's not even interested in Katie's pictures of Lovey's rescue. Poor bird! She was badly injured when she was found in the woods, and now—well, she looks as happy and healthy as a green frog with a full belly!

Katie says she'll be ready to release in the wild any day now.

"Woo-oo-oo-oo!" Lovey coos.

I'm hoppy for Lovey. But I also remember when I first came to Room 26 and the young tads debated whether they should return me to the wild or keep me at school.

I'm glad I stayed, but I still long for the wild life in the swamp. The long days catching crickets, learning lessons from Granny Greenleaf and having jumping contests with my best pal, Jumpin' Jack.

I miss the mud and the mucky water, the assortment of tasty insects and my friends and family.

I miss floating on a lily pad on the sun-dappled water.

But in the end, a wildlife expert said it's not a good idea to return frogs to the wild because of diseases. She also said frogs are highly endangered, which is terrible news. Who can imagine a world without frogs?

Still, I'm rooting for Lovey. I really am. It's hard seeing a bird not able to fly.

Brad is not impressed. "Why do we talk about birds all the time? There are lots more interesting things to do," he mutters. "At my old camp, we were looking at bear tracks!"

I try to tune out his bragging now. (I learned how to do that back in the swamp with the bullying bullfrogs.)

On the positive side, Ms. Mac encourages Gail to put down her pen and offers to walk her to the next session.

As soon as they leave, Humphrey launches into a stream of squeaks. He's clearly angry, and I'm pretty sure what he's upset about is Brad's attitude.

Humphrey squeaks so much, even Lovey speaks up. Her

"woo-oo-oo-oo" is soothing, but I think she's saying, "Quiet down over there!"

Humphrey finally gets the message.

🐾 🐾 🐾 🐾

That night, when Humphrey and I are taken to the dining hall, it's still raining.

"The campers are disappointed we won't have a campfire tonight," I hear Katie tell Ms. Mac.

"Wait till they see what we have planned!" Ms. Mac says.

The rain makes the grass greener and the mud muddier. Everything smells wilder tonight. If only I could get out of my tank and feel the glorious drops hit my skin.

Back at the dining hall, there's a lot going on besides eating.

It's about as noisy as a summer night in the swamp, where there's chirping, buzzing, wing flapping, hooting and howling, not to mention the deafening RUM-RUMs of the bullfrog chorus.

This room is full of giggling and belly laughs, clinking and clattering, shouting and singing and lots of loud talking. Humphrey and I take it all in from our position on a table near the stage.

I observe a lot from there: Gail is still sulking while the other girls are busy chattering. The boys are having what I think is a burping contest. If they are, Simon will definitely win first prize. He's a talented burper!

I also see Ms. Mac pull Miranda aside to talk. Since we're in a quiet spot, she leads her near our table.

"Miranda, have you been writing your mom positive letters about camp, like I suggested?" Ms. Mac asks.

Miranda nods. "Oh, yes. Every day I tell her how much I love it here, how nice the other kids are and how good the counselors are."

"That's good." Ms. Mac nods. "I heard from your mother again today, and she thinks you sound a little down in your letters."

"I'm not!" Miranda says.

I know from being in Room 26 that Miranda doesn't lie.

"I guess she's just worried," Ms. Mac replies. "Did you tell her how much you'd like to try horseback riding?"

Miranda nods again. "Yes! I told her that the instructors have been teaching riding for years and the horses are gentle. I told her how much the other girls like it. I even told her about Golden being my favorite horse. She's super gentle, and her name is the same as mine!"

That's right, Miranda's full name is Miranda Golden. Perfect!

Ms. Mac smiles. "I believe you. I just needed to check. I'll keep trying to think of ways to encourage her not to worry so much."

"Good luck with that." Miranda shakes her head. "I don't think she'll ever stop worrying about everything I do."

"She'll always worry because she loves you, Miranda," Ms. Mac tells her. "You know that."

By now they've walked away, and I can't hear them anymore.

"What do you think of that?" I ask Humphrey. He doesn't answer.

I think of how happy Miranda would look horseback riding. I think of how happy Golden would be if Miranda were riding her.

But I'm not sure what to do about it. At least not yet.

I have no time to think about Miranda now, because I spot A.J. standing nearby with Garth and Ty.

I'm not surprised when Ty challenges A.J. a bit. I have a few brothers like that.

When Ty says the Blue Jays are going to have to work a lot harder to beat the Bobwhites in the Clash of the Cabins, that sounds like normal kidding around.

But I'm as confused as a mosquito in a windstorm when Garth's tone turns nastier.

I am used to Garth and A.J. being best friends and doing almost everything together. I am *not* used to seeing Garth trying to needle A.J.

"Yeah. We've *already* beaten the Blue Jays," Garth tells him. "You might as well admit you guys are losers."

He acts more like a bullying bullfrog than the Garth I know from Room 26. Yes, Aldo did say, "Believe it, and you'll achieve it," but I think Garth is taking that advice a little too seriously!

They bicker back and forth, but there is no winner in this war of words. It's a stalemate, which ends when Mrs. Wright blows her whistle in an ear-piercing shriek that sends campers squealing with their hands over their ears.

Things settle down when Hap Holloway takes the stage and speaks into a microphone, which makes his voice boom. He's as loud as Mrs. Wright's whistle!

"Welcome to the Happy Hollow Comedy Club!" he says.

Then the counselors take the stage, and I can't believe my froggy eyes. The grown-ups are acting out silly little plays they call "skits," and the campers can't stop laughing.

I can't quite follow all of it, but I do enjoy seeing Aldo wearing bunny ears. I never saw a rabbit with a big, floppy mustache like Aldo's before!

I look around and see everybody having such a good time.

Gail's smiling for the first time since she got to camp, and Miranda seems to have forgotten all about her mother.

Even Garth looks more like the friendly boy I remember from Room 26.

I've been worried about their problems, but tonight, it looks like those problems have disappeared.

On the other hand, Brad and Noah don't smile at all, no matter what the counselors do.

Later in the evening, I end up in the Bobwhites' cabin. They must be doing a great job of cleaning the cabin and being on time to win me again.

Sam is still his upbeat, confident self. When Ty compliments him on the home runs he hit today, Sam smiles and says, "Thanks." In return, he compliments Ty on his diving.

"I'm still learning," Ty admits.

"Well, you nailed it today," Sam says.

Hearing that makes me hoppy.

"I'm trying to get in a little extra batting practice so we can win the Clash of the Cabins," Sam continues. "I think if we practice for all of the events, we might have a chance."

"*Chance?*" Garth says. "We've got to win! We can't lose with you on our team, Sam!"

"How about volleyball?" Sam says. "We could work together on our serves."

Garth sits back and crosses his arms. "It doesn't matter how I play. With your scores, we can't lose."

"There are some events we haven't practiced much," Ty says. "Like knot tying and archery."

Noah looks up from the book he's reading. "Knots? You need to look at these charts. It's all right here." He holds up the book so we can see pictures of all kinds of knots. "We could practice right now."

Ty sighs. "I don't know. My brain understands the knots, but my hands don't get the message."

"You guys aren't listening," Garth says. "Stop worrying. We've already got this wrapped up!"

Sam shakes his head. "It's not over yet."

"We're going to win. I guarantee it," Garth insists.

"I want to win, but I don't think I want to meet the Howler," Ty admits.

Again, Noah says there's no such thing as the Howler. "I'd know about it," he explains.

"I read this comic book about a swamp monster," Sam says. "He was all mossy and smelly and swampy."

That sounds good to me!

"I think the scariest thing is his howl." Garth lets out a chilling "owoooo!"

The way he does it, it's blood-curdling, all right.

"Owoooo! Owoooo!" Sam and Garth howl together.

Noah rolls his eyes, which isn't surprising, but Ty claps his hands over his ears.

"Guys . . . stop!" he says. "I'll have bad dreams."

"It's *not real*," Noah tells him. "You guys would believe anything."

He sounds definite, but I'm not so sure myself. I haven't seen a Howler, but there are a lot of things I haven't seen that are real, like gravity and electricity.

There *could* be a Howler, but I hope Noah is right.

That night, it stops raining. It's eerily quiet as the boys

sleep soundly, but I stay awake, listening for a distant "owoooo!"

I hope Ty isn't having bad dreams. I hope *I* don't have bad dreams. And I wonder if Humphrey is worried about the Howler. Has he ever seen such a fearsome creature before? (I have, if you count owls, bats, snapping turtles, wolves and hawks.)

Then I remember Granny Greenleaf's words. "It's wise to be wary of things that are scary."

I go to sleep feeling wary and thinking of my song.

Where's the Howler?
Where's the Howler?
In the woods.
In the woods.
I don't want to see him.
I just want to flee him.
Stay away!
Stay away!

Furry Worries

. . . .

If your buddy is in trouble, go
to help him on the double!

—Granny Greenleaf's
Wildlife Wisdom

I don't know if he's trying to tell me about the Howler or something else, but Humphrey is unusually excited, even for him. He squeaks out a long story while we're in the rec room.

"SQUEAK-SQUEAK-*SQUEAK*! SQUEAK-SQUEAK-*SQUEAK*!"

"Calm down, Humphrey! You'll get a sore throat!" I tell him.

He doesn't get to finish his story because Katie and Ms. Mac set some boxes next to us on the table. They say that the boxes contain stickers.

The only stickers I've seen grow on bushes in the swamp,

and believe me, if you get close to them, you'll definitely get stuck! But these stickers are harmless-looking little pieces of paper with pictures on them.

Katie and Ms. Mac quickly leave.

I expect Humphrey to try to finish his story, but he does something unexpected instead. He flings open his cage door and dashes across the table.

I am as surprised as a butterfly landing in a bramble bush to see this, because I'm pretty sure Ms. Mac said they'd be right back.

"Hurry! You'll get caught!" I warn him.

Humphrey grabs some stickers in his mouth, hurries back to his cage and swings the door shut.

Now what? If Katie and Ms. Mac come back, they'll have a pretty good idea that he's been out of his cage. How else would he have gotten those stickers?

As usual, he has a plan. He races across the cage, pokes his head behind his mirror, pulls out the notebook he keeps hidden there and stuffs the stickers inside.

Just as Ms. Mac and Katie return, he slides the notebook back in its hiding place.

ꓦ ꓦ ꓦ ꓦ

Later, in the Nature Center, Humphrey watches two of the campers intently.

"It's not polite to stare," I tell him, but he ignores my boings.

What's so interesting about Gail and Brad? They hardly ever smile. And they both hate camp.

Whoa! I guess that's what they have in common!

After a while, everyone in the center leaves for a nature hike, which sounds good to me. I'd like to see the sky above, feel the grass below and maybe even get a little muddy instead of being stuck inside. No such luck.

Humphrey squeaks at me, then races over to his hidden notebook, pulls out some stickers, opens the cage and scurries down the leg with the stickers in his mouth.

I guess he must know what he's doing, but what if the nature hike is a short one?

"Hurry, pal!" I call.

He heads straight for Brad's notebook, which is on the floor, and slides a sticker under the cover.

Then he dashes over to Gail's notebook and slips the other sticker in it.

There are no blinds here, so there's no cord for him to swing on. So, to get back, he scrambles up a tall plant next to Jake the Snake's tank.

"Don't get too close to Jake!" I warn him.

Jake sticks out his tongue, but Humphrey ignores him and races back to his cage.

Whew! He makes it! I dive into the water side of my tank and swim some laps to calm down.

Then I take time to Float. Doze. *Be.* That's when I let my mind drift wherever it wants to go.

Today my mind wants to hop back to the swamp for a nice, juicy cricket. But when I hear Katie say, "Open your notebooks," I leap back onto my rock to see what happens.

When Brad and Gail open their notebooks, they both look surprised at what they find.

Humphrey squeaks with happiness as they both put their stickers in their pockets.

I'm still puzzling over what just happened when the next group of campers comes in for their session.

As soon as he arrives, Noah marches over to our table, leans down and makes a big announcement. "I'm going to try to get you out of that cage, Humphrey. You too, Og."

Humphrey squeaks in alarm, and I suddenly feel as cold as the day before hibernation.

"NO!" I boing. "Not a good idea!"

Sure, I'd do okay in the wild, but I don't think poor Humphrey would have a clue.

Noah goes right to his seat and waves his hand. Ms. Mac calls on him.

"Can't we at least let Humphrey get some fresh air?" he asks.

Ms. Mac points out that one entire wall of the cabin is open, so there's plenty of fresh air.

"He could walk around in his hamster ball," Noah suggests.

That sounds harmless enough, as long as Humphrey stays inside.

Before I know it, my furry friend is rolling along the floor, under chairs, past shoes, and . . . wait a second. He's rolling right out the door!

"BOING!" I say. I wish I could just say, "HELP!"

Am I the only one who notices?

I keep my eyes peeled, watching to see Humphrey roll back in again. But Humphrey doesn't appear, and class goes on as usual. Sometimes I'm amazed at how much humans miss!

So I try again. "BOING-BOING!"

No response. This calls for stronger measures. "BOING-*BOING*!"

No one raises an eyebrow. Not even Noah. And he thinks he knows it all.

I wait a few seconds and then try again. "BOING-BOING! BOING-*BOING*! *BOING-BOING!*" I warn.

Katie suddenly stops talking. "Og, what's the matter with you?"

"THERE'S NOTHING THE MATTER WITH ME!" I tell her. "It's Humphrey I'm worried about!"

Ms. Mac finally notices. "Oh! Where's Humphrey?"

"HE ROLLED OUTSIDE!" I boing as clearly as I can.

Of course, they don't understand. They waste a lot of time searching inside, when I know Humphrey is *outside*.

FINALLY, they catch on.

"Maybe he rolled outside," Miranda says.

"Of course," Noah agrees. "I knew he wanted to be outside."

"But he has no idea what he's doing in the wild!" I insist.

Nobody's listening to my boings. They have all rushed outside to look for Humphrey.

I wish I could roam free, because I think I could find him faster than the big tads will.

I hold my breath and wait. When I finally hear Simon say, "Wait a second! I see him!" my heart leaps up in my chest.

Before I know it, Humphrey is safe and sound back in his cage again.

"Welcome back, pal," I tell him.

He staggers into his sleeping hut and doesn't come out for a long time.

While Humphrey is sleeping, Ms. Mac talks to the class about how everyone is responsible for our animals and how we should have been paying more attention to Humphrey.

"I am as guilty as the rest of you," Ms. Mac says. "We all have to keep our pets safe."

"Yes!" I agree. "Keep Humphrey safe in his cage!"

"He's not a pet!" That's Noah, of course. "He belongs in the wild. And that's where he wanted to go."

Did he? Really? That doesn't sound like Humphrey.

"Thank goodness Og was paying attention and let us know," Ms. Mac says. "And he certainly did let us know."

Yes, but it wasn't easy!

While I float on my back in the water and wonder what happened to Humphrey out there, I remember my song and think about a new verse.

Humphrey loves to help his friends,
He's a daring camp pet,
But once he rolled right out the door,
And I got really upset.

Humphrey Hamster, let me know,
Everywhere that you've been!
Tell me what you did out there
So I can rest again!

I'm going back to the Robins' Nest again tonight, and I have mixed feelings.

I'm hoppy to have a chance to find out if Miranda's mom is letting her try horseback riding and if Gail has cheered up. But I'm worried that any minute, Lindsey will grab me and give me a squeeze. Ewww!

Ms. Mac delivers me to the cabin before dinner. During that time of day, the campers rest a little and write letters. Of course, Gail has been writing letters nonstop since she arrived at Camp Happy Hollow!

I keep a close eye on her today, and right away, I notice

her take out that sticker and look at it, before quickly stuffing it back in her pocket.

Do I see a hint of a smile on her face?

The girls all sit on their beds with paper and pens in hand.

"Maybe I'll write to Og," Lindsey says.

"Why?" Kayla asks. "He's right here."

Lindsey giggles. "I'll write him a love letter."

Kayla rolls her eyes. "Lindsey, he's a *frog.*"

"I know," Lindsey says. "But he's so cute. Maybe I'll write my parents and see if they'd let me bring him home when camp is over."

Miranda objects. "He's *our* class pet. You can't take him!"

"But you have Humphrey, too. Not fair!" Lindsey says. "But okay, I won't write about taking Og home."

That's a huge relief to me!

Miranda brings her paper and pen over to my table. "Mind if I sit here, Og?" she asks.

"Please do!" I answer. After all, if Miranda sits next to me, maybe Lindsey won't pick me up and give me a hug.

Miranda thinks and writes. She writes and stops to think. She crumples up her letter into a little ball.

"Oh, Og," she says. "I write the same thing every day. I tell Mom I love camp. I tell her it's fun and safe. I tell her how great the counselors are. And I tell her it would sure be fun to try riding a nice, tame horse. I even told her about

Golden, who the youngest campers get to ride, but nothing ever changes."

"I know!" I tell her. "I'm so sorry!"

Miranda takes out another piece of paper and stares at it. "She means well, Og. She loves me and wants the best for me," she says. "But you'd let me ride a horse, wouldn't you?"

"Of course!" I boing.

Personally, there's no way *I'd* ever ride a horse, but then . . . frogs never do.

"Dear Mom," Miranda says as she writes. "I miss you, but I love camp more every day! I've made so many new friends."

"BOING!" I tell her. "That's a good start."

"I know you don't want me to go horseback riding, but everybody is having fun on their rides . . . except me."

Hmmm. I don't think her mom will like that.

"BOING-BOING! BOING-BOING!" I say, splashing around in the water.

Miranda pulls her paper back. "Og! You're getting my letter wet."

"Sorry." I use my softest boing. "It's just a bit boring!"

Miranda stares hard at my tank. "I guess it sounds a little boring. I keep saying the same thing over and over."

I hop up onto my rock so we can look at each other eye to eye. "BOING-BOING!" I say to let her know I understand.

"I wish *you* could write the letter." Miranda giggles. "But you'd get the paper all wet."

An excellent point. A frog trying to write a letter is not a good idea.

Miranda sighs. "Just tell me what to say, Og."

I know she's kidding, but I decide to give it my all. "BOING-BOING. BOING-BOING! BOING-*BOING*!" I tell her.

She giggles again. "I can't write BOING-BOING. Mom wouldn't understand."

"BOING-BOING-BOING-BOING-BOING!" I keep trying. *"BOING-BOING-BOING-BOING-BOING!"*

"Oh! It's silly, but it might work," she says as she picks up the pen and starts writing.

I hope she doesn't write what she hears, but what is in my heart.

"Dear Mrs. Golden, I hope you don't mind me writing, but I am Og the Frog, and I am a good friend of your daughter's," she says out loud as she writes.

BING-BANG-BOING! She's got it!

"I'm keeping a close eye on Miranda here at Happy Hollow, and I can see she's having a good time," Miranda continues. Then she crosses something out.

"I can see she's having a GREAT time." She smiles. "She's made so many friends and loves all of her activities."

"You've got it!" I tell her.

Miranda writes some more. "She's a nice girl. She obeys all the safety rules whatever she does."

Good point! And it's true.

"But I know she feels left out because everyone is taking horseback riding lessons except her," she says. "The instructor here, William, has been teaching riding to campers for over ten years. He even teaches five-year-olds when he's not at camp."

Miranda stops writing.

"Keep going!" I say. "Write what's in your heart."

Miranda stares at me. I know all she's heard are my boings.

Then she writes more and reads it to me. "There's a horse that I'd love to see her ride. Her name is Golden, like Miranda's last name. She's beautiful and is the gentlest horse here."

She stares at the letter. Something is wrong!

"Og, do you know how to spell *gentlest*? It doesn't look right." Miranda crosses something out and reads again. "She's beautiful and is the most gentle horse here."

That sounds better, and it's easier to spell.

Miranda writes some more and reads it back to me. "Even animals get to try new things at camp. I have learned to live in peace with a bird and a snake. And Humphrey the Hamster has gotten used to life in the great outdoors."

Nice touch!

"Thanks for being a great mom," Miranda continues. "Lots of love, Og the Frog."

I'm hopping with happiness. "Perfect!" I say.

Miranda is still deep in thought. "It needs something more."

"No, it's *perfect*." I hop so high, I almost pop the top off my tank!

"Don't get the letter wet, Og," Miranda says. She's right, of course, so I settle down.

Miranda writes some more. What more is there to say?

When she's finished, she puts down the pen and reads to me: "BOING-BOING! BOING-BOING!"

"The perfect touch," I tell her.

I do love Miranda, and I'm hoppy I could help her.

I just hope the letter *works*.

🐾 🐾 🐾 🐾

Later, when the girls head to bed, Lindsey stops at my table to say good night.

"Good night, Oggie-pie," she says.

I've been called Og, Oggie, Bongo and recently a cutie. Dr. Okeke, who once visited Room 26, said my scientific name is *Rana clamitans*. But Oggie-pie? This is a first.

"Sweet dreams," she continues.

I breathe a sigh of relief. She's going to bed!

"I'm going to kiss you good night," Lindsey says.

"No! No! Absolutely not!" I leap into the water to get away from her.

Lindsey giggles. "Nighty-night," she tells me. Then she

kisses her finger and taps it against my tank and heads back to her bed.

Whew! That was a close one!

But I stay in the water most of the night in case she comes back.

Stuck

· · · · · · · · · · · · · · · ·

Mud may make you feel just
ducky, but getting stuck in the
muck is downright yucky.

—Granny Greenleaf's
Wildlife Wisdom

The next morning in the Nature Center, I am relieved to see that Lindsey isn't in the first group. I need a break from her.

Then I hear Noah's voice close to my tank.

"Og, I found your true home," he tells me in a soft voice. "You need water—lots of it. And other frogs to be friends with. I'll help you, don't worry."

I wasn't worried before he spoke to me, but I am plenty worried now!

"Don't do me any favors!" I tell him with a series of loud boings.

Class begins, but I can't concentrate because I'm think-ing about what Noah said. Sure, I like being near water and having frog friends. But he forgot to mention the bad things, like Chopper, who is always waiting for a nice, plump frog to pass by. Or the water moccasins, who look asleep even if they aren't. Then there are owls, hawks and other flying enemies. It's not all sunbeams and lily pads, I can tell you!

Once Ms. Mac and Katie take the campers on a nature hike again, Humphrey and I are alone in the classroom, and I have time to think.

For months now, my true home has been Room 26 of Longfellow School, right next to Humphrey.

We both have challenging jobs as classroom pets. Instead of spending most of my days dodging enemies, I try to be encouraging to the big tads in the class. I help Humphrey keep track of the time when he's out of his cage . . . which he is right now!

Leaping lizards! He's doing it again. He's sliding down the table leg with *more* stickers in his mouth. While I've been daydreaming, he's been trying to help Brad and Gail. I don't understand how his plan works, but I know he has one.

"Hurry, Humphrey!" I yell.

Again, he tucks stickers in each of their notebooks, then climbs the tall plant—which sways alarmingly—up to the table and back to his cage.

"You did it!" I say. I don't think he hears me, because he's already spinning on his wheel.

Once again, when the campers return to their desks, Brad and Gail find the stickers. But this time, they actually speak to each other! What progress! Soon the two of them are laughing and chatting away.

Humphrey stops spinning and looks over at me. "SQUEAK-SQUEAK-SQUEAK!"

"I saw it, Humphrey! Your plan is working!" I say.

Then he crawls into his sleeping hut for a well-deserved nap.

I'm back with the Bobwhites that night. That makes me as nervous as a toothless fox . . . because Noah is a Bobwhite.

Tonight, he's pretty quiet, just scribbling on a notepad. I hope he's writing home, not working on a plan to get Humphrey and me released into the wild!

Garth and Ty happily celebrate Sam's recent successes. He has already broken camp records in softball home runs, volleyball and swimming.

"We can't lose!" Garth says. "Not with Super-Sam!"

Sam shakes his head. "Everybody has to do their best, okay? It's not all about me."

"But we've nailed it already!" Garth seems ecstatic. "A.J.'s group doesn't have a chance!"

I must admit, it does *look* as if the Bobwhites are impossible to beat. But there's something about Garth's attitude that bothers me a lot.

"I think the point of the Clash of the Cabins is for all of us to give it our best," Sam says.

"My best in sports isn't good enough," Garth says. "A.J. has always beaten me at everything. I'm counting on you, Super-Sam! We're going to see the Howler! Owoooo!"

This time, the other Bobwhites don't join in.

Ty stares at the floor. "I want to win, but do we *have* to meet the Howler?"

"That's the whole point," Garth says. "What do you think, Noah?"

Noah looks up from his scribbling. "Statistically, I think we'll win."

Garth gives him a thumbs-up. "Thanks! We're *in*!"

I'm glad when Sam changes the subject. "Guys, we should think about our skit. Any ideas?"

I don't really listen as they toss out ideas and discuss them. All I can see is Ty still staring at the floor. I think he's seriously afraid of the Howler. And to tell the truth, so am I.

But the next night, as I watch the Chickadees hard at work on their skills for the Clash of the Cabins, I don't think *they're* afraid of anything!

I'm amazed to watch Abby lead them in tying knots. She works at the speed of a fly-catching frog's tongue.

She's also made a huge chart about all the signs used in trail marking. No one works harder than the Chickadees. Abby is a strong leader who keeps the other girls focused on the Clash of the Cabins.

Not that I don't hear a few complaints.

"Abby, I think we're supposed to have fun at camp," Marissa grumbles.

"Sorry," Abby says. "We've had enough practice for tonight. But you do want to win, don't you?"

"Yes!" the other girls agree.

After lights-out, the girls usually talk quietly in the dark for a while before going to sleep. But tonight, they fall asleep right away. And so do I.

The next morning in the Nature Center, I'm still thinking about the Howler when Miranda and Kayla come in to talk to Ms. Mac about a surprising subject.

"We were thinking maybe Noah is right," Miranda says.

"Eeek!" Humphrey squeals. I know how he feels.

Miranda says she hates seeing Humphrey cooped up in the Nature Center and wants to give him a tour of the camp.

"Well . . ." Ms. Mac says. "Yes, I guess so. As long as you *promise* not to let him out of his cage."

"What about *me*?" I wonder. "BOING-BOING?"

"Oh, Og, it's too hard to give you a tour," Ms. Mac says. "The water in your tank would be sloshing the whole time."

"We still love you," Miranda tells me.

I'm glad they love me, but when the campers and Humphrey leave for their tour, I feel alone and left out.

And I am worried about my friend. After all, Ms. Mac

made me promise to watch over Humphrey. What is she thinking now?

I float in the water for a while. That always makes me feel better.

Soon I find myself singing a brand-new but somewhat sad song.

Humphrey's having a journey,
Humphrey's having a journey,
Humphrey's having a journey,
While I am stuck right here.

I am stuck right here!
I am stuck right here!
Humphrey's having a journey,
And I am stuck right here.

I'd like to go out exploring,
I'd like to go out exploring,
I'd like to go out exploring,
Instead of being stuck.

I don't like being stuck!
I don't like being stuck!
I'd like to go out exploring . . .
But I am stuck right here.

Being stuck is not a great feeling, so to clear my head, I decide to do a workout. I don't get as much exercise in my tank as I did in the swamp, but I try to stay in shape.

First, I splash as hard as I can. Then I hop on my rock for a series of jumping jacks. Up, down, up, down, up, down, up, down, up, *done*. I've moved on to swimming laps in my tank when Simon and Ty rush in, giggling.

"I can't believe she took it off," Simon says. "I figured she slept with it on."

"And showered with it on." Ty laughs.

I can't believe they sneaked out of the nature hike!

"Where can we hide it?" Ty asks.

"Someplace where she won't find it for a long time," Simon says. "I missed the perfect save in volleyball today. When she blew her whistle, I blew the play."

I don't think they realize I'm watching, so I freeze and float silently in my tank.

"Why don't we throw it in the lake?" Ty asks. "Then she'll never find it."

Simon shakes his head. "No, that's too mean. This is just a harmless prank. We'll hide it for a while. We can always give it back later. That'll confuse her!"

"Hey, over there!" Ty points to a small cabinet with narrow drawers. "I've never seen anyone open that."

They rush over and start opening drawers. "There are a lot of photos in here," Simon says. "Katie and Ms. Mac might go in there to take them out for class when we're not around."

They continue to look around until Simon points at our table. In fact, he looks like he's pointing to Jake the Snake. "Look! There's a little space under his terrarium."

Simon and Ty race to our table. Sam pulls something out of his pocket, and now I know what they're talking about: Mrs. Wright's silver whistle. Like the boys, I am amazed. I didn't think she ever took it off, either.

That whistle is something I dread. I get nervous when Mrs. Wright walks into the room just because there's a chance she might blow it. Poor Humphrey's little ears wiggle, and he squeals with pain when she uses it.

And my ears (the skin over them, really) quiver like a thin reed on a windy day.

"I'll slide it under there," Simon says as he pushes the whistle under Jake's terrarium.

"Go!" Simon yells, and they run outside.

Well! That was surprising!

Of course, the boys broke several camp rules, but I admit, a few days without the blasts of that whistle would be welcome.

Still, however they got it, it doesn't belong to them. Maybe I should help give it back? I think I could pop the top of my tank and hop on over there, but I'd hate to get caught out of my tank. The campers will be back any second.

I'm still thinking of the right thing to do when Miranda, Kayla and Sayeh bring Humphrey back to our table.

"SQUEAK-SQUEAK-SQUEAK!" My buddy sounds excited.

"That Noah—why does he want to free the animals?" Sayeh asks.

"AMINALS," Miranda says. "He can't spell very well!"

"Humphrey and Og are our pets," Sayeh says. "Can you imagine Humphrey out in the wild?"

"No, I can't!" I boing.

"Jake and Lovey would probably do okay. And Og would probably be all right," Miranda says. "But not Humphrey."

"EEEK!" my furry friend squeaks. I don't blame him. It's something I've worried about ever since we arrived at Camp Happy Hollow.

After the girls leave, Humphrey squeaks wildly, trying to tell me what happened, but I still have no idea.

And what's an AMINAL? I think about that while I float in the water and finally decide that I am. At least if you're a poor speller.

At last, Humphrey crawls into his sleeping hut.

The poor guy is exhausted. He needs a good nap, and I need time to think. It's been a very confusing day so far!

Unexpected Journey

· · · · · · · · · · · · · · · ·

Once you step into the Great
Unknown, it's not unknown
anymore.

—Granny Greenleaf's
Wildlife Wisdom

At night, Aldo takes Humphrey and me to the dining hall to see the cabins perform their skits in the Comedy Club.

"You don't want to miss this," he tells us. "It's going to be a lot of laughs."

But before the fun begins, Hap Holloway makes a serious announcement. "There were signs that went up today about freeing our animals," he begins.

The signs were about freeing the *aminals*, according to Miranda, but no one corrects Hap.

He explains that Lovey *is* going to be released into the wild.

My heart pounds because up until a few months ago, *I* was a wild thing. Is he going to say the same thing about me?

Then Hap Holloway says that Humphrey and I are different because we are pets. "They are not to be released into the wild. They are only on loan to us. Understand?"

And then an amazing thing happens. Half of the campers start chanting, "Hum-phree! Hum-phree!" The other half chant, "Og! Og! Og! Og! Og!"

Nobody ever did that back in the swamp. (Of course, my name was Bongo then.) I may be cold-blooded, but I feel warm inside when I hear them.

But I'm as cold as the ice when the pond freezes over when I hear the earsplitting shriek of a whistle! It's Mrs. Wright, and yes, she has a whistle! I'm amazed that she found it so quickly. How did she think to look in that little space under Jake's terrarium?

"There will be order!" she says, and everyone quiets down. The whistle works, even though it sounds a little different to me.

Before I know it, the skits begin, but I must admit, my mind is still on that whistle.

While the Blue Jays are on the stage acting something out, I'm trying to figure out how Mrs. Wright found the whistle. I never saw her come in.

I glance up at the stage, where Richie and some others are pretending to be a train.

Mrs. Wright blows her whistle again as part of the skit, and this time, the crowd cheers.

Maybe I'm the only one who notices that unlike the silver whistle Ty and Simon hid, this one is black. It's not the same whistle, but it's as loud as the other one.

I'm afraid the boys' plan didn't work, but Simon and Ty are laughing and don't seem to mind.

When the audience cheers, I send out a few loud boings as well.

I have trouble concentrating on the Chickadees' skit because I'm still thinking about the whistle. It was wrong of Simon and Ty to skip out on the nature hike. I guess the counselors didn't notice, but like Humphrey, they didn't grow up in the wild like I did. They shouldn't be roaming around by themselves.

And it was wrong of them to take Mrs. Wright's whistle, even if it was just a prank.

But there was no harm done, so why do I feel funny about the whole thing? And I don't mean *funny* like laughing, which the audience is doing at the end of the Bobwhites' skit.

I mean *funny* like an odd feeling that things are not right. That's why I'm having trouble paying attention.

But when Miranda suddenly grabs Humphrey's cage and hides him behind the curtains onstage, she gets my *full* attention. What in the swamp is going on?

Now it's the Robins' turn to put on a skit.

I keep my eyes glued to the stage, but I can't see Humphrey. They've set up a fake door onstage. They take turns opening the door just a little and then running away screaming about a monster.

I think they enjoy pretending to be scared.

Finally, they call on Ms. Mac. When she opens the door, she shrieks, too. When she starts to run away, she flings the door open wide so all of us can see what's behind it— Humphrey's cage!

So, Humphrey is the horrible scary monster!

Of course, everyone roars with laughter at the idea that anyone would think my furry friend is a monster! The crowd cheers, "Hum-phree! Hum-phree!"

The girls are all smiles as they high-five each other. Even Gail.

To show him how much I enjoyed his part in the skit, when Humphrey returns to his place next to me on the table, I dive to the bottom of my tank, then leap out of the water and onto my rock, shouting, "Way to go, Humphrey! You're a star!"

It's been such a wonderful evening, I don't think about that whistle again.

ꕷ ꕷ ꕷ ꕷ

The girls in the Robins' Nest cabin can't stop talking about the success of their skit.

"We ought to get some serious Clash of the Cabins points for it," Kayla says.

The other girls agree.

"We might get more horseback riding points than we thought," Miranda announces. Her eyes are sparkling. "My mom gave me permission to ride, and I had my first lesson today. I got to ride Golden!"

The other girls seem as surprised as I am.

"Yippee!" I boing.

"Miranda, that is so great!" Gail gives her friend a hug. This is a different Gail than just a few days ago. "What made her change her mind?" she asks.

Miranda hesitates and then replies, "Our friend Og here wrote her a letter that convinced her it was okay."

The other girls laugh. "Sure, Og wrote a letter," Kayla says.

"He must have used waterproof ink!" Lindsey jokes.

"Well, that's my story, and I'm sticking to it," Miranda says. "And Og knows it's true."

BING-BANG-*BOING*! I certainly do. Not that I deserve the credit. But I did inspire Miranda to write a different kind of letter.

"That's my Oggie-pie!" Lindsey heads over to look at me more closely. "The bestest little froggy-woggy in the world!"

I wince at the Oggie-pie, but right now, I feel like I am a pretty good little froggy-woggy.

ꝡ ꝡ ꝡ ꝡ

The next morning, Kayla drops me off at the Nature Center. Except for Jake and Lovey, I am the only one there until Katie runs in with her arms full of books.

"Morning, team," she says cheerily, plopping the books down on the desk. "It's getting busy around here! It's the last day to prepare for the Clash of the Cabins!"

She's stacking the books when Mrs. Wright comes in.

"Katie, I just realized I never looked in here for my whistle," she says. "Have you seen it?"

Katie smiles. "I see it right now. It's around your neck."

Mrs. Wright shakes her head. "Hap loaned me this whistle, but I still haven't found the silver one. I'd sure like to have it for the events tomorrow."

I guess one whistle isn't just like another.

"Oh," Katie says. "I haven't seen it, but please look around."

Mrs. Wright starts to search the desk and drawers. "I know it seems a little silly, but that whistle has a special meaning to me."

It has a special meaning for everyone at camp, too. A feeling of pain and irritation!

"You see, that whistle belonged to my mother," Mrs. Wright explains. "She was a PE teacher, too. I followed in her footsteps because I admired her so much. Since she's gone, I hardly ever take it off."

I never even thought of Mrs. Wright having a mother!

"Well, let's find it, Ruth," Katie says.

Sometimes, when she blows that whistle, it's hard to believe Mrs. Wright has a heart. But now I know she does . . . and it's aching.

"It's under Jake's tank!" I shout. "I'm sorry I didn't tell you!"

Mrs. Wright and Katie continue to search the room . . . in all the wrong places.

"It's under Jake's terrarium!" I boing even louder.

"Calm down, Og." Katie turns to Mrs. Wright. "I wonder what's bothering him."

"I know where it is!" I try again.

"I have an idea," Katie says. "Let's try the dining hall again."

Soon the two of them head out the door and the room is quiet again.

꙰ ꙰ ꙰ ꙰

All of the campers are serious about preparing for the Clash of the Cabins. I can hardly keep up with everything they are practicing. Volleyball and softball sound like a lot of fun, but I wish I could join in the swimming competitions! I wouldn't care about winning—I just want to be in the water!

Of course, if they had a leaping contest, I don't think anyone could beat me, unless my old friend Jumpin' Jack showed up.

꙰ ꙰ ꙰ ꙰

All the practicing and anticipation must have worn out all of the campers, because every single Bobwhite falls asleep early that night. But one of them didn't sleep very long—Noah. It's barely even light out when he comes over to my tank. And why is he carrying a bowl of water?

"The coast is clear, Og." He reaches in and picks me up. Luckily, he doesn't squeeze me. "I'm taking you on a big adventure!"

He hurries out the door with me in the bowl, and I struggle to keep my head above the waves to see where we're going.

I wanted an adventure in the wild. I guess I'm about to have one.

Noah moves quickly down the path that soon becomes a narrow trail through the woods. "You're going to love this, Og," he says. "I'm taking you to a place you'll like a lot more than sitting in a cabin all day."

That sounds frogtastic, but did he ask permission? Did he tell anyone he was taking me? Or am I being frognapped again, the way I was when I was taken from the swamp?

Going on an adventure isn't fun if it's not *your* idea.

Noah picks up his pace, and we seem to be going downhill. All around us, I see a blur of green.

The blur suddenly turns into a forest of tall trees.

"Here it is, Og," Noah says. "The perfect spot for a frog."

The waves calm down, and I peek over the side of the bowl. All I see are trees until I turn and look behind me at one of the most beautiful pieces of water that I've ever laid my froggy eyes on.

"It's Lake Lavender," Noah says.

BING-BANG-*BOING*!

The lake is sparkling, and I can hear the gently lapping water, a choir of birds singing, bees buzzing and something else. There's a distant chorus of "BOING-BOING! BOING-BOING!"

Snakes alive! There's a large group of green frogs out there, and they are singing a peppy song.

Hoppy, hoppy,
This is a hoppy day!
We're so hoppy,
Hoppy in every way.

We spend our days eating crickets,
And playing in the thickets,
And so we say
In every way
Oh, this is a hoppy day.

I guess I'm not the only green frog that likes to sing! It's a simple song, but you can't beat the message.

"Hear those frogs, Og? They sound like you. This is where you belong." Noah sets me in the tall grass. Gently, thank goodness.

"Doesn't this feel better than sitting in a tank in a classroom?" Noah asks.

I don't answer because just then, a warm breeze fans the grass. It makes me as hoppy as the singing frogs.

"Breathe in that fresh air," Noah says.

I do.

"Look up at that big blue sky," he adds.

I do.

"Let me find you some mud so your skin won't dry out." He picks me up and moves me into a shallow puddle of water.

Oh, joy! I do love mud and muck!

"Thank you," I say. "BOING-BOING!"

"You deserve some time in the wild," Noah explains.

I gaze out and see the wide expanse of water. The grass around me is so full of flies and butterflies, crickets, mosquitoes and dragonflies, I think my heart will burst. (And maybe my stomach after I catch as many as I can.) Memories of McKenzie's Marsh flood my brain.

I feel like I'm at home.

Froggins and Friends
· · · · · · · · · · · · · · · · ·

There's always room in the heart
for a new friend.

—Granny Greenleaf's
Wildlife Wisdom

Suddenly, the chorus of green frogs gets louder.

"Who goes there?" it asks. "Green frog, who are you?"

The frogs sound friendly enough, but I can't see them because I'm still far from the water, and there's so much tall grass between me and the lake.

"Green frog, where are you?" they all boing. "Are you friend, or are you foe?"

"Friend!" I say, hoping they are friends in return.

"WE CAN'T HEAR YOU!" the chorus shouts.

I take a few leaps closer to the lake.

I hear Noah's voice. "Og? Og!"

"I AM OG," I yell in my biggest boing. Then I realize

that Og is the name *humans* call me. In case any of my old swamp friends are out there, I add, "But my real name is Bongo! I came from McKenzie's Marsh!"

There is silence for a moment, and finally, they answer. "WHO ARE YOU, OG? WHERE ARE YOU?"

I guess none of my old friends are here after all.

I take a few more hops through the tall grass but stay low so they can't see me . . . yet.

"Og! Og! Og! Og!" they chant.

"I come in friendship," I reply. "FRIENDSHIP!"

I hear footsteps behind me. "Og? Come back. I need to take you back to camp," Noah says.

"Just a few seconds more," I say, even though he can't understand me. I take several large leaps toward the lake.

"Og? Where are you?" Noah calls out.

He sounds much farther away. I guess I took more leaps than I thought.

"Please come back, Og." Noah sounds worried, but I'm listening for the calls of the green frogs and enjoying the gentle breeze swaying the tall grass around me.

"This is Lake Lavender!" the frogs cry out.

Off in the distance, I hear Noah. "Og, show me where you are!" He sounds frantic.

Suddenly, I am almost at the edge of the lake. Cool blue water stretches before me as far as I can see.

I should go back now, of course. Back where Humphrey

and all my human friends are waiting. But for now, it's strange and wonderful to speak and be understood again! After I catch a glimpse of these green frogs, I'll hoppily hurry back to Noah.

"OG!!!!" Noah sounds desperate, but his voice is muffled, while the green frogs sing out loud and clear.

> Welcome, welcome, to you,
> Welcome, welcome, to you.
> Og, tell us your story!
> Welcome, welcome, to you.

I take one more giant leap. Splash! My toes are in the cool, delicious water of Lake Lavender.

A fly buzzes by, and I grab him with my tongue. Yum!

Suddenly, I am eyeball to eyeball with a large green frog, who says, "Can I help you?"

And I don't hear Noah at all.

"Hello," I answer. "What's your name?"

"I am Froggins Frog," he says.

"I'm a frog, too," I tell him.

Froggins chuckles. "I already know that. But tell us, where have you come from?"

"I come from pretty far away. I guess you'd say I'm from the Great Unknown," I explain.

"Ahhh!" the frogs all exclaim.

"At least that's what we called it back in McKenzie's Marsh," I continue. "Right now, I'm staying at the camp up the hill."

Froggins's eyes shift as he gazes up the hill. "*Humans* live there. Frogs and humans don't mix."

Way back in the swamp, I guess I believed that, too. But not anymore.

I change the subject. "Nice lake you have here. It's the biggest one I've ever seen."

"It is the *only* lake." Froggins sounds awfully sure of himself. Doesn't he know there's a great big world out there?

I don't want to argue with him, so I change the subject again. "Where are your friends? I heard them singing."

There's a rustling in the grass behind Froggins.

"Step up, frog family. It is safe," he says.

The other green frogs take a step closer.

"Are you sure, Froggins?" one frog timidly asks. "Who is he? How did he get here?"

"Come and ask Og for yourself," Froggins tells the group. "Can't you see he's our brother? Where are your manners?"

The whole group hops closer, but they stay well behind Froggins.

"Welcome, Og," they say in a chorus.

"Thank you," I say. "I guess I'm lost. And my skin feels dry in this hot sun."

Froggins hops into the water, and I follow.

BING-BANG-BOING, it feels good! Why didn't anybody tell me there was such cool and refreshing water so close to camp? With such a variety of tasty snacks!

Ah, my skin starts to soften, and I feel like my old self again.

The green frogs just stare at me as I float in the water.

I'm not sure what they find interesting about watching me float. After all, they're frogs that float, too. But as Granny Greenleaf likes to say, "If the waters are calm, don't make waves," so I try to relax. Float. Doze. *Be.*

I also listen for Noah's voice, but I haven't heard it for a long time.

After a while, I get bored, so I hop back up on shore. "Thanks," I tell Froggins. "I feel a lot better."

The other green frogs gather around me in a circle. They still can't take their eyes off me, even though we all look pretty much the same.

"Brother Og, may we ask you some questions?" Froggins says.

I tell him they can ask anything they want.

"Why did you come here?" one shy frog asks in a soft boing.

"I guess you'd say it was an accident," I explain. "I didn't plan on coming here."

"You said you were up the hill, with the humans," another frog asks. "But how? Humans are not our friends."

I pause before I answer, because I don't think they'll

believe me. "Many humans—and other creatures—are friends to *me*."

The shy frog shivers. "That is unnatural."

"You see, Brother Og, we try to stay away from humans. For most of the year, Lake Lavender is beautiful. In the spring, everything turns green, and there's plenty of food. In the fall, the world turns red and gold, and there is so much beauty to behold," Froggins explains.

I nod in agreement. "I know it well."

"In winter, we sleep peacefully," Froggins continues. "But in summer . . . *they* come and invade our beautiful Lake Lavender."

I'm pretty sure I know who he means by *they*.

"Splashing, swimming, running over nests and disturbing homes with their canoes and heavy paddles, stealing our fish, sometimes killing our delicious insects," he says. "They are barbaric."

What he says is correct, and yet I know how kind humans can be as well.

Every species intrudes on other species. That's just the way it is.

I must be careful in my answer. I don't want to upset them. "That's true. And yet many humans have been extremely kind to me. They have welcomed me into their homes."

There's a huge gasp from the green frogs gathered around me.

"You, Brother Og, are a rare frog, unlike any I have ever met," Froggins says. "You have wisdom that goes far beyond the lake. Beyond the hills. Beyond the sky."

I wouldn't exactly call what I've learned at Longfellow School, in human homes and at camp wisdom beyond the sky, but I guess it is wisdom beyond this lake.

"No, I'm a just regular frog who has had some unusual experiences," I say. "And I can't say that all humans are bad. In fact, right now there are some humans who are probably worried about me."

The campers! I've been so wrapped up in froggy conversation, I wasn't thinking about my friends. They must know I'm missing by now. They'll be out looking for me.

They might even come back to the lake for me! My heart lifts a little thinking of that.

I imagine their worried faces: Miranda, Sayeh, Richie, Garth, Ms. Mac, Katie.

And I imagine another small and worried face: Humphrey's. He gets upset when anything goes wrong for a friend, and he's done so many favors for me.

"It is hard to believe there is kindness in humans," Froggins says.

"I have other friends, too," I admit. "Like my furry little friend, Humphrey."

The green frogs of Lake Lavender hop away from me in horror.

"Fur?" one of them says. "Fur is bad."

"Anything furry is our enemy," another frog agrees.

Some of what they say is true. Bears, wolves, foxes . . . I'd steer clear. But not Humphrey. All I can tell them is, "Not always."

The green frogs whisper to one another, then one steps out of the circle, closer to me.

"Brother Og, now we know who you are," she announces. "We have longed to meet you for so long, and we are honored you are here."

Longed to meet *me*? They didn't even know about me until today.

She continues, "Each night we watch you up in the sky, twinkling at us. Each night we sing to you."

Froggins nods. "You have heard our song. Thank you for honoring us with your presence."

I'm as mixed up as a mosquito in a snowstorm.

I start to explain that I'm not from the sky, and then I understand. When my friends and I used to look at the stars at night, old Uncle Chinwag would point out a group of stars in the sky. If you use your imagination, it looks something like a frog.

Then Uncle Chinwag would tell us a story. "Since ancient times, it is said that the stars that make up the Star Frog at night are real frogs during the day. They drop to earth to roam across great lands and learn about the earth. When the sun goes down, they leap back up to the sky to share their stories."

A Star Frog sounds something like the great frog explorer, Sir Hiram Hopwell. But somehow, this group thinks I *am* one of those frogs.

I don't have time to object, because they begin to sing in beautiful harmony.

Hello, Star Frog, how are you?
Hope you're hoppy; we are, too.
Someday may you leave the sky,
Stay with us a little while.
Tell us how it feels to light
The dark sky up every night.

Dear friend Star Frog, you are wise,
From your perch up in the skies.
Tell us what you think and see,
Tell us what it's like to be
A great Star Frog, up so high,
Sending greetings from the sky.

"And here you are," Froggins says when they finish. "Thank you for coming."

"Thank you, Star Frog." The other green frogs bow. "We are honored."

To be polite, I bow back, even though I know I'm no Star Frog.

"We would like to show you the rest of the lake," Froggins says. "Will you join us in a group swim?"

I'm always up for exploring, and this will be my chance to see something new. Even the famous frog explorer, Sir Hiram Hopwell, probably never saw Lake Lavender.

"Sure!" I say.

And we're off!

Humans might not know that some frogs don't like to swim very much. In fact, tree frogs and others like them spend almost no time in the water. And they still call themselves frogs!

But green frogs, like me, and bullfrogs (the less said about them, the better) love to be in the water. So to us, there's nothing more fun than a group swim.

We must look like a giant green wave as we make our way across the lake.

And oh, what a lake it is!

Lily pads and logs, weeping willows almost touching the water, and everything around the lake is the color of a green frog!

I do see a snake or two and remember the dangers back in McKenzie's Marsh.

"Do you have snapping turtles here?" I ask Froggins.

"Never heard of them," he answers, and that's good news to me. I don't have to worry about one of Chopper's relatives lying in wait in the water.

From the sun, I can tell it's afternoon now. We stop to rest at the opposite bank of the lake from where we started.

I manage to catch three juicy flies and six little mosquitoes and am eyeing a tasty dragonfly when I hear a far-off sound that's somehow familiar.

"Humans!" Froggins says. "Lie low."

Humans! That's good news to me.

"Luckily, they're on the other side of the lake," Froggins observes.

That's bad news to me.

The human voices are distant, and I can't quite make out what they're saying.

Is it "Frog! Frog!"? Or could it be "Og! Og!"?

If I could get closer, I might get found and taken back to camp.

As nice as Lake Lavender is, I'm ready to go back to camp, to my friends . . . and especially to Humphrey.

"I think I'd better get back," I tell Froggins.

"I understand," he replies. "After all, you have to return to your place in the sky by tonight."

I'd like to set Froggins and his friends straight on who I actually am, but I'm not sure they'd believe me. I'm also anxious to return to camp.

"Let's go!" I say. And we start swimming.

The way back to our starting place seems to take a lot longer than the swim to the far shore.

We swim and swim and swim some more.

The sound grows closer. *Pitter-patter. Pitter-patter.*

I plan my escape from the Howler. I'll dive in the water and swim away. But what if the beast can swim?

I suddenly wish I *could* be a Star Frog and magically escape to the sky.

The noise grows closer. What are those squeaks? Does the Howler wear squeaky shoes?

I back up into the shallow water, prepared to dive deeper at any moment. I haven't been so scared since I woke up from a nap in the swamp and was looking straight into Chopper's massive jaws!

At last I hear it. That unmistakable sound. The sound I've heard a thousand times in Room 26.

"SQUEAK-SQUEAK-SQUEAK!"

My ears must be playing tricks on me, but I hear it again!

"SQUEAK-SQUEAK-SQUEAK!"

It's impossible, but just in case, I shout, *"Humphrey?"*

The answer is immediate. "SQUEAK-SQUEAK-*SQUEAK*! SQUEAK-SQUEAK-SQUEAK-SQUEAK-*SQUEAK*!"

"I'm here, Humphrey!" I shout. I know he can't understand me, but maybe he'll hear my boings.

I take a few hops forward, and I see his tiny silhouette in the moonlight. It's Humphrey, looking so small, so furry and so brave.

I leap closer, and yep, it's him all right.

"Humphrey! How'd you find me?" I ask.

But then I see dozens of tiny eyes blinking in the dark. I

Sometimes I hear a faint echo of "Og! Og!"

And then I don't. I guess the campers stopped looking for me.

By the time we get back to shore again, the human voices have stopped, and I'm exhausted. After all, I've spent the last few months swimming in a small tank, so I just had quite a workout.

The sun is low in the sky, and there's a new but familiar sound: a loud chorus of bullfrogs.

"Rum-RUM-RUMMMM! *RUMMM! RUMMMM! RUMMMM!*"

I guess bullfrogs are pretty much the same everywhere.

The sky darkens, and in between the bullfrogs' rumming, I hear the sweet song of the crickets.

"Look up!" Froggins suddenly says. "It's night . . . but the Star Frog isn't there. Proof that Og is a Star Frog."

I look up and don't see stars of any kind because it's cloudy. But I'm even more sure than ever that I couldn't convince these frogs I'm *not* one of the Star Frogs if I tried.

I move away from the group, to the shore of Lake Lavender.

Then I remember about the Howler. He's out there somewhere in Haunted Hollow. And Aldo said that's on the lake. Will I hear his horrible cry any second now? Will my blood curdle?

I sit and listen. There are many different night sounds made by frogs and other creatures.

QUANK-QUANK-QUANK!

RUM-RUM-RUM!

TUCK-A-TUCK-A-TUCK!

CHIRP-CHIRP-CHIRP!

Nothing I haven't heard before. Nothing even close to blood-curdling so far.

I'd like to head back to camp, but I don't know the way. While I'm not thrilled about spending the night anywhere there might be a Howler, I really don't want to get lost in the woods!

10

Unexpected Rescue

· · · · · · · · · · · · · · ·

Unexpected friendships are often the best.

—Granny Greenleaf's
Wildlife Wisdom

I still hear QUANKs and loud RUMs, CHIRPs and TUC̶ A-TUCKs. I don't hear human voices, though.

Did the campers give up when I didn't answer the calls? Has Humphrey already forgotten me and all the goc̶ times we had?

Or does Humphrey miss me, but he's stuck in his ca̶ in some cabin at Camp Happy Hollow?

Hours pass without any sign of the Howler.

But there is a new sound: a strange rustling in the ta̶ grass. Something is moving toward the lake. I can see tl̶ stalks rippling in the moonlight.

Is the Howler approaching? I hear a *whoosh* in the gras̶

think Humphrey must have gotten some small, furry wood-land creatures to help guide him. And I was worried that he couldn't take care of himself in the wild!

"I missed you, pal!" I say.

"SQUEAK-SQUEAK-*SQUEAK*!" he answers. Of course he missed me! Why else would he risk the dangers of the wilds of Camp Happy Hollow to find me?

"WHOO-WHOO. WHOO-WHOO!"

There's an owl nearby. The throng of tiny field mice suddenly crowd around us.

"*Squeak-squeak-squeak,*" they tell Humphrey in tiny voices, and we all move to the cover of the brush.

Back in the swamp, I didn't pay much attention to field mice. Just like Froggins said, nonfurry creatures don't hang out with furry things in the wild.

Yet these mice helped Humphrey find me. And now they surround us and start moving up the hill.

We are silent, except for the rustling of the grass.

In the distance, I hear the green frogs calling. No, I'm wrong. They're singing their Star Frog song.

Thank you, Star Frog, and bye-bye.
Have a safe trip to the sky.
We will see your twinkling beams,
Anytime the full moon gleams.
In the future we will share
Stories of a frog so rare!

I look up at the sky. The clouds have drifted away, and there it is: the Star Frog up in the sky.

Well, at least I gave them some good stories to tell.

※ ※ ※ ※

It's a long way back to camp, but I'm impressed with how fast Humphrey can run through the grass. I guess all that wheel spinning has paid off.

But I keep a close eye on my furry pal. After all, he's never been in the wild at night before. He has no idea of what dangers are out here. I'll bet he thinks that ripple in the grass ahead of us is just the sound of the wind . . . but I'm certain there's a snake in our path. And frogs and small furry creatures are just what he's looking for!

(That's why I'll never really trust Jake.)

"Follow me! This way!" I boing, and hop off to the left to make a wide circle around the snake in the grass.

I hope it isn't Jake.

Luckily, Humphrey and the mice follow, and the rippling fades and disappears.

When we reach the steps of the Robins' Nest cabin, the mice and I are quiet, except for Humphrey and a cute little mouse squeaking back and forth.

They must understand each other. It sounds like they are special friends.

As the mice skitter away into the night, I thank them.

"BOING-BOING!" I say, hoping they understand what I mean.

"SQUEAK-SQUEAK!" they answer. Maybe the wild mice figured out I saved them from a snake.

"SQUEAK-SQUEAK-SQUEAK!" Humphrey adds. I wonder if he knows I helped him.

It was a long trip through the grass, and my skin is feeling dry.

Thoughtful as always, Humphrey leads me to a nice puddle of water, and I plop right in.

We sit there together for the rest of the night, but when it starts to get light, Humphrey squeaks something to me and then slides back under the cabin door.

I know Humphrey. He has some sort of plan.

So I sit and wait, loving the feeling of nice, gooey mud on my skin.

I may have dozed off, but I jump when the loud wake-up music blares. I can hear the girls moving around the cabin, but it takes a minute before I hear a piercing hamster squeak.

There are footsteps, and then Miranda shouts, "Humphrey! You're out of your cage!"

In a flash, Humphrey is sliding out the door again. Miranda is right behind him as he scampers down to the puddle where I am waiting.

"Og! That's Og!" Miranda screams.

The other girls are outside now, squealing happily as Gail gently scoops me up and Miranda runs off to tell Ms. Mac.

Soon Humphrey's in his cage and I'm back in my tank.

Ms. Mac thinks one of the girls left the cage door open. "And you, Humphrey, were naughty to get out of your cage," she tells my friend.

But I know the truth. My best buddy is a true friend and a brave hero.

And no matter what Froggins said, sometimes a furry creature can be a frog's truest, most trusted friend.

After all, we are both wild things.

Everybody cheers when Humphrey and I are carried into the dining hall. I guess they missed us!

Noah stands up and apologizes to me. "I thought I knew a lot about animals," he says. "I thought that frogs belonged with frogs. But now I know some frogs belong with people."

Some frogs belong with hamsters, too.

Hap sends the campers off for the final events of the Clash of the Cabins.

Katie takes my tank, telling Humphrey, "I think Maria is preparing some special treats for you." She adds, "You look a little skinny today. I'll come get you in a little while."

Who wouldn't look skinny, walking all across Camp Happy Hollow and back on those tiny feet?

"Eat up!" I tell him.

At the Nature Center, Katie places my tank on the table. "The campers will be coming in most of the day to take their nature tests, so we'll have to be quiet."

"Fine with me!" I boing back. I've had quite enough excitement for a while.

I hear Hap Holloway on the loudspeaker calling for Katie to come to the dining hall for a short meeting.

"Oh, I forgot!" she says, and dashes out of the Nature Center.

The room is completely silent after she leaves. Jake and Lovey are napping.

I'd like to Float. Doze. *Be.* For a while, at least. But strangely enough, I keep glancing over at Jake the Snake's terrarium and thinking of Mrs. Wright's beloved silver whistle hidden under there.

It will take a few minutes for Katie to get to the meeting. Even if it's short, the meeting will last awhile, and then it will take her a few more minutes to get back to the Nature Center.

I'll be taking a big chance, but I decide to go get the whistle and pull it out into the open, where some human will surely see it.

It doesn't take me long to pop the top off my tank. I've had a lot of practice doing that!

I hop down to Jake's terrarium. It's a lot like my tank, but it's lower and wider and there's no water in it, only tree branches and leaves.

I see his beady eyes watching everything I do. I sure hope he can't pop the top off *his* tank! I try not to look at him.

Hunkering down to look at that little space under the terrarium, I see a problem. I can't fit under there, and I can't reach it with my legs. I glance around to see if there's something I can use to push or pull the whistle out. There's nothing helpful on the table, and if I go search the rest of the room, I will surely get caught outside my tank again!

"Ssssss," Jake hisses. I glance up and see that he looks restless and a little hungry.

I'm about to give up and go back to my tank when I remember I have a secret weapon that most other creatures don't have: a long and powerful tongue that's attached to the front of my mouth instead of the back.

Pretending that the whistle cord is a cricket in the marsh, I whip my tongue out as fast as I can, grab the cord and pull it toward me.

Success! I hook the cord under my back legs and drag it back to my spot on the table. My plan is to leave it right outside my tank where no one can miss it.

Then I stretch out my legs and leap as high as I can, right into my tank, landing with a mighty splash.

The splash is different than usual because my plan didn't work out as I expected. The cord was wrapped around my back leg, and now the silver whistle is in the water with me! No wonder my back leg felt so heavy.

It's too risky to try to take it out again because Katie may come back at any time. The best I can do is to push it to the front of the tank. Someone will see it there—I hope.

I hop up on my rock and sing.

There was a swamp where lived a frog
And Bongo was his name-o.
B-O-N-G-O.
B-O-N-G-O—

My song is interrupted when a surprising trio enters. It's Mrs. Wright, and she's with Simon and Ty!

"We thought we were being funny, Mrs. Wright," Simon says. "But when Katie announced how important that whistle is to you, I felt terrible."

"Me too," Ty adds.

"It wasn't a funny prank, was it? But I appreciate you boys stepping forward and admitting what you did," Mrs. Wright says.

BING-BANG-BOING! They did the right thing after all!

"The whistle's over here." Ty rushes over to Jake's terrarium and slides his hand in the space under it.

He looks shocked—and why shouldn't he?

"It's not here!" he says.

Simon joins him and reaches under the terrarium as well. "It has to be! This is where we hid it."

Mrs. Wright takes a ruler out of the desk and pokes it around under the tank. "Maybe it's stuck," she says.

"It's not stuck!" I tell them. "It's over here—in my tank!"

They don't pay attention to my boings.

"Boys? Are you sure you hid it here?" she asks.

"Yes!" they answer.

"But it's over here now!" I hop up and down on my rock. "In my tank!"

"What is Og so excited about?" Mrs. Wright asks. "You'd think he wants to tell us something."

Ty comes over to my tank. "Quiet down, Og. We can't hear ourselves think."

"The whistle is here!" I repeat.

Simon and Mrs. Wright move over to my tank as well.

"Something must be wrong," Mrs. Wright says. "What is it, Og?"

"Look in the water!" I tell them.

Mrs. Wright turns to the boys. "Do you think he's sick?"

Simon bends down so he's eye level with me. "He looks all—oh! There it is!"

BING-BANG-BOING! He's pointing at the whistle.

Mrs. Wright gasps. "It's my whistle! How on earth did it get in there? Are you boys playing another prank?"

"No, honest we're not," Simon says. "I'll get it."

"Be careful not to disturb Og," Mrs. Wright says.

Believe me, I don't mind being a little disturbed if she can get her whistle back!

Once the whistle is rescued, Mrs. Wright dries it off on her shirt, then stares at it lovingly.

I didn't mean to pull a prank, but it turned out to be a pretty good one!

Clashing Cabins

· · · · · · · · · · · · · · · · ·

A true winner knows the only
real competition is yourself.

—Granny Greenleaf's
Wildlife Wisdom

Throughout the day in the Nature Center, one thing is
clear. All the campers can think about is who will win
the Clash of the Cabins.

When Garth comes in to take his nature quiz, he doesn't
look as confident as he has been. In fact, he looks about as
gloomy as a vulture with an empty stomach.

"Did you hear? Super-Sam has poison ivy—a lot of it!"
Garth says.

"Eeek!" Humphrey squeaks.

I had noticed Sam scratching his arms a lot at breakfast.

"The nurse says Sam won't be able to compete in most
of the events," he says. "Nobody wants to touch the things
he's touched."

I don't know who's suffering more, Sam or Garth.

Sayeh comes in to talk to Humphrey, while Garth hangs around my tank.

"I wish I'd practiced harder, but now it's too late," he admits.

"Think positively!" I remind him.

"I wish I hadn't bragged to A.J. so much," Garth admits. "Without Super-Sam, we're *definitely* going to lose to the Blue Jays. But there's nothing I can do."

"It's never too late to try!" I tell him. "Give it your all! Give two hundred percent!"

To encourage him, I dive into the water and swim fast laps. Believe me, I make quite a splash.

"Hey, Og, you're getting my glasses wet," Garth says.

I hop back up on my rock and do some fantastic leaps. "Reach for the stars!" I tell him, hoping that he'll work a little harder in volleyball.

"I wish I could leap like you, Og," Garth says. "I'd be a better volleyball player."

"Hop to it!" I shout. "Just be as fast as you can be!"

Garth chuckles at my antics. It's good to see him grin. "I wish you were on my team," he says.

As he walks to the desk to pick up a test, I realize that I'm on everyone's team at Camp Happy Hollow. I know they all can't win, but everybody can try!

Then I hear a familiar voice say, "Oggie-pie! How's my cutie-wootie today?"

As Lindsey leans in close to my tank, I stay silent. Maybe if I don't respond, she'll call me by my real name.

"I brought you a treat," she says.

Yum! To me, a treat is a cricket, a fly or even a meal-worm.

My mouth waters, until she drops a round thing with red and white stripes around it right into my tank. That's no insect!

It slowly sinks to the bottom, and I see the water around it turning pink.

Yuck!

"It's a peppermint," she tells me. "See how much I love you?"

Noah rushes up to the tank. "What are you doing? He doesn't want that. Don't you know anything about animals?"

"It's just a peppermint," she says.

"It's not good for him or Humphrey," Noah says as he races to Katie's desk and picks up a little net with a long handle.

"I'll take it out." Lindsey pushes back the lid of my tank and starts to stick her hand in, but Noah stops her.

"Don't," he says. "Your hand is probably full of germs. You'll contaminate the water. You don't want to hurt Og, do you?"

Lindsey looks as if she's going to cry. "Noooo," she wails. "I *love* Og."

Noah fishes out the peppermint and says, "Aw, don't cry.

I'm sorry I got upset, but even if they're pets, animals are still animals. They don't eat the same things or live like we do."

"I never had a pet," Lindsey says. "I always wanted one."

"Well, if you ever do get one, you need to learn how to take care of it," Noah tells her. "Hey, there's a great book about frogs here in the rec room. After the test, we can clean his tank, and I'll show you if you want. It has cool pictures."

Lindsey wipes away a few tears. "Thanks. I'd like that."

She turns to me. "I'm sorry, Og."

"It's okeydoke," I tell her.

And I'm glad that she's going to read that book. The sooner, the better! In fact, I wouldn't mind having a look at it myself.

ॐ ॐ ॐ ॐ

I am as jumpy as a nervous jackrabbit in the dining hall later that night, waiting to see how the campers will react when they find out which cabin won the competition.

When Garth rushes in, he hurries over to my tank. "Og! We tied for second place in volleyball! I was leaping around like, well, like *you*! And I finished third in swimming!"

"Way to go!" I tell him. "BOING-BOING-BOING-*BOING*!"

The room gets unusually quiet when Hap Holloway stands up to make the announcement.

He doesn't say who won, at least not first thing. He says

119

the Robins came in third and the Bobwhites and Chickadees tied for second place.

There's plenty of cheering, and I see Garth smiling. Miranda is smiling, too, because she got second place in horseback riding . . . with Golden, of course.

And Abby and the Chickadees won first in knot tying. I'm not a bit surprised.

Then comes the big announcement. Hap says, "And in first place, the winners of this year's Clash of the Cabins competition: the Blue Jays!"

A.J. starts jumping up and down, chanting, "Blue Jays rule! Blue Jays rule!"

There's even more cheering when Hap announces a special award is going to Sam for his great athletic abilities.

Sure, the Bobwhites would have won if Sam didn't have poison ivy, but they gave it their all and tied for second place.

Suddenly all the anxiety and competition among the cabins is over. Chickadees and Robins are hugging, and Brad and Richie are laughing with Noah. Best of all, Garth tells A.J. he's sorry for the way he acted. I'm hoppy to see Garth and A.J. shake hands.

"It's all over now," A.J. says. "And you outplayed me in volleyball."

Lindsey leaves the excited crowd to visit me. "Og, I'm going to try to find you a real treat tomorrow—a *cricket*! Noah's going to help me."

Noah may have put me in danger by releasing me at Lake Lavender, but he's more than made up for his mistake now.

🐾 🐾 🐾 🐾

That night Humphrey and I stay in the cabin with Ms. Mac, Katie and Mrs. Wright. I'm hoppy to see that shiny silver whistle hanging around Mrs. Wright's neck. And yes, she does sleep with it on!

After such an exciting day, I look forward to a good night's sleep, and I get it.

Good thing, too, because the next day, all the campers—not only the Blue Jays—are howling, "Owooooo!" all day long.

Our time in the Nature Center gives everyone something else to think about besides the Howler, because a stranger shows up.

He is a veterinarian from the wildlife refuge.

"Meet Dr. Singleton," Katie says. "He's the vet who helped us fix Lovey's wing when she was rescued."

"And today he's here to see if she's healed enough to be released," Ms. Mac adds.

The vet examines Lovey carefully and says, "She looks completely healed."

The campers cheer.

Katie rushes off to make an announcement to the whole

camp while the vet answers questions about doves like Lovey. I am hoppy to hear that they mostly eat seeds, unlike hawks and owls, who eat small creatures like frogs and little furry things.

Then Dr. Singleton meets Humphrey and me. He must be a smart doctor, because he takes one look at me and says, "Ah, *Rana clamitans*."

"That's me!" I answer.

I hear Katie's voice on the loudspeaker, saying that anyone who wants to see the release should come to the Nature Center. Before long, every single camper at Happy Hollow shows up.

After Ms. Mac assigns Sayeh, Brad and Noah to assist in the release, they take Lovey's cage outside.

"Good luck, Lovey!" I shout after her.

Then Miranda grabs Humphrey's cage and rushes out.

"Hey, wait!" I shout. "BOING-BOING! BOING-BOING!"

I know it's easier to transport Humphrey's little cage than my tank, but I really want to see the release. Instead, I'm stuck here with Jake the Snake.

Luckily, there's a window behind me, and I see the crowd outside huddled around in a circle, but I can't see Lovey.

I keep my eyes on the group and watch Sayeh step out of the circle, carefully holding the bird.

She sets her on the Nature Center porch, and Lovey

spreads her wings. Yep, her injured wing is healed, all right. Without hesitation, she flaps her wings and begins to hop.

Dr. Singleton nods and says something. Sayeh picks up Lovey and carries her away from the building to an open space as the crowd watches from a distance. Unfortunately, they block my view of Lovey again.

I manage to get a glimpse of Sayeh handing the bird to Noah. That's a nice thing! Even if he made a mistake in taking me to the lake, he cares a lot about animals.

The crowd blocks my view again, but then I see Lovey in the air, flapping her wings and rising quickly, stopping on a high treetop.

BING-BANG-BOING!

After a while, she takes off again, flying higher and higher until she's a silhouette against the blue sky.

A cheer breaks out as she disappears.

"Lovey took off, Jake," I say. "She's free now." I'm not sure he's interested, but he has lived next to Lovey for a long time.

The crowd huddles around again, talking. I can't hear what they're saying. They all raise their hands.

Then Brad and Noah come into the Nature Center.

"Jake, we all voted to release you into the wild, too," Noah tells him.

I can hardly believe my eyes, but it's true! They pick up Jake's tank and carry it outside.

I don't get to see the release because the crowd huddles around his tank, but after a while, there's another cheer.

I'm glad Jake is free. His tank seemed a little small for him. And I'm not that sad to see him go.

When Humphrey's cage is back on the table beside my tank, he excitedly tries to explain what he saw. "SQUEAK-SQUEAK-*SQUEAK*!"

"I know, pal," I tell him, because for once I understand exactly what he says.

The Haunted Howler

. . . .

*Every day is the start of a new
adventure.*

—Granny Greenleaf's
Wildlife Wisdom

Things are quiet for the rest of the afternoon. Humphrey
and I are in the rec room as it turns dark. The Blue
Jays—including A.J., Richie, Simon and Brad—are pacing
outside, and I don't blame them. They are about to meet the
Howler!

Many of the other campers are gathered in the rec room,
and they aren't as excited.

"They won fair and square," Abby says. "But I'm still a
little jealous."

Ty is the only one who is in a good mood. "I'm not. I
don't want to meet that Howler thing."

"I do," Garth says. "But I'm happy that A.J. is going. After
all, he's my best friend!"

"I still don't think there's such a thing as a Howler," Noah says. "But I could be wrong. Right, Og?"

"We all make mistakes!" I boing back.

Ms. Mac comes in and says, "Everybody but the Blue Jays—attention! I'm taking you all to town to see a movie!"

"Will it be scary?" Ty's voice is shaky.

Ms. Mac smiles. "Maybe . . . in a fun way," she answers.

Soon the room is empty except for Humphrey and me. We watch and wait.

When a small bus pulls up in front of the rec room, Hap opens the door. "Okay, Blue Jays. All aboard for Haunted Hollow!" I hear him say.

Aldo and some of the other counselors also get on the bus.

Just before they leave, A.J. suddenly runs in and picks up Humphrey's cage. "Hap Holloway said it was okay." He sounds happy and excited.

"Good luck!" I shout after my pal, but he's gone.

I'm all alone in the rec room and feeling a little sorry for myself.

Of course, unlike the Blue Jays, I've already spent the night at Lake Lavender. And the funny thing is, I didn't hear anything that sounded like the Howler. Curious, isn't it?

Still, when the Howler sees humans, he might come out of hiding.

I stop feeling sorry for myself, and I think about

Humphrey. If there is a Howler, my buddy might be scared. He might even be in danger! I wish I could be there to help him the way he helped me.

"Feeling lonely, Og?" a voice says.

It's Aldo's wife, Maria. She plops down on the couch near my table. "You're not the only one left behind."

"Hi, Maria!" I greet her.

"I had to prep breakfast for tomorrow. But we're not entirely left out," she says. "The windows are open, and I have an idea that you and I might get to hear the Howler from here."

She certainly believes there is a creature called a Howler.

Maria opens a book and begins to read.

I relax and slide into the water. Time to Float. Doze. *Be.*

A long time passes, and I'm getting worried about the Blue Jays. It's almost too quiet out there, so I sing softly to myself.

Where's the Howler?
Where's the Howler?
In the woods.
In the woods.
I hope my friends don't see him.
I hope my friends can flee him.
Stay away!
Stay away!

Maria stops reading and stares at me. "Og, you're a singer! No one told me that! I'm glad I stayed behind so I could hear your song."

I'm glad she did, too.

Now it's quiet except for the chorus of crickets outside. They wouldn't be singing if *I* were out there!

And then I hear it—a faint but definite "owoooo!"

"BOING!" I say. "Wow!"

Maria jumps out of her chair. "You heard that, Og? That's the Howler."

I think of Humphrey—so small, so nervous, so out of place in the woods.

"Owoooo!"

Yep, it's the Howler, but it's not as eerie as I expected.

Truthfully, it sounds like many little Howlers. There are a lot of voices howling, and they all sound young.

They sound familiar.

They sound like kids!

Maria chuckles. "I hope Aldo is taking pictures," she says. "I'd like to see the looks on the Blue Jays' faces when they find out who the Howler is."

"OWOOOO! OWOOOO!"

"What's going on?" I ask Maria.

And then I hear a new sound: laughter. The laughter echoes through the woods, and we can hear it all the way up here.

"Oh, I'll tell you, Og. Those campers didn't go to a movie. Ms. Mac took them to Haunted Hollow, where they all hid in the woods and pretended to be the Howler. It's a camp tradition to prank the Clash of the Cabins winners."

Another prank! But this one is a lot funnier than taking Mrs. Wright's whistle.

Best of all, my pal Humphrey is perfectly safe.

It's late when the campers return, laughing and chatting.

"It was just a little scary," Ty says with a big smile. "But in a fun way!"

"SQUEAK-SQUEAK-*SQUEAK*!" Humphrey tries to explain. "SQUEAK-SQUEAK-SQUEAK-SQUEAK-SQUEAK-SQUEAK!"

"It's okay, Humphrey," I boing back. "I knew it all the time."

※ ※ ※ ※

The next day is quiet and relaxed. The campers get to sleep late, and so do Humphrey and I. Humphrey dozes in the rec room for much of the day, and I must admit, I do, too.

From time to time, some of the campers come in to play games or visit us. I'm so hoppy to see that Garth and A.J. are best friends again and Sam isn't scratching his arms as much. Brad looks happy playing cards with Richie and Simon, and Gail is once again the giggliest girl in the room.

Noah and Lindsey look at the frog book together, and Abby and Miranda go on a last horseback ride. The horse trainer, William, takes a picture of Miranda on Golden and gives it to her.

That last night, there's another awards ceremony in the dining hall. Humans sure like to give out awards!

There are so many prizes, I lose track. Gail is the Funniest Camper, which I wouldn't have predicted when she first arrived. A.J. is the Loudest Camper, which doesn't surprise me at all.

Sam even gets an award for the Itchiest Camper, and Brad is named the Most Improved Camper.

But when it comes to the award for Most Popular Camper, Hap announces a tie . . . between Humphrey and me!

Best of all, the prize turns out to be treats for both of us, and Lindsey presents me with a cricket! *And* she calls me just plain Og.

Then . . . it's over! I hear Hap telling the campers that is was a great session, and he hates to see it end.

END? END!

First school ended, and now camp is ending?

This is sad news, and I know my pal Humphrey feels the same way, because his whiskers wilt and he crawls into his sleeping hut. I understand.

I get one more night back with the Chickadees. There's no knot tying, but there is lots of dancing like chickens and telling ghost stories. Ms. Mac even lets them stay up a little late.

I will miss Camp Happy Hollow.

🐾 🐾 🐾 🐾

The next morning, from our place on the rec room table, I see what happens when camp ends. The same parents who left their children here not long ago return to pick them up.

All the suitcases, boxes, backpacks and duffel bags are loaded back into cars. There are hugs and presents and good-byes . . . and then the campers are gone!

It's as quiet as a snake lying in wait. Even Humphrey doesn't squeak for the rest of the day.

As night falls, Ms. Mac pays us a visit.

"I hope you two had a good rest today," she says. "Because your work isn't over. Tomorrow, a whole new group of campers arrives for the *next* session of camp!"

Leaping lizards—Humphrey and I are going back to work! Only this time, we'll know so much more about the schedules, the pranks, the Clash of the Cabins . . . and the Howler!

And I'll know that Humphrey can manage quite well in the wild, with a little help from a friend like me.

Later in the evening, the counselors gather in the rec room to recall the high points of the first session.

Then Maria brings in popcorn, Katie takes out her

guitar, and Ms. Mac gets her bongo drums. The counselors and Hap sing for the rest of the evening. When I hear those drums, I have to join in the fun as well.

There was a swamp where lived a frog
And Bongo was his name-o.
B-O-N-G-O!
B-O-N-G-O!
B-O-N-G-O!
And Bongo was his name-o.

And in a camp there lived that frog
And Bongo was his name-o.
B-O-N-G-O!
B-O-N-G-O!
B-O-N-G-O!
And Bongo was his name-o.

I dedicate the next verse to the best friend a camper ever had: Humphrey.

A hamster came to camp as well
And he's a wild thing now-o.
HUM, HUM, HUM, HUM-PHREY!
HUM, HUM, HUM, HUM-PHREY!
HUM, HUM, HUM, HUM-PHREY!
And Humphrey is his name-o.

And I'm not that surprised when a tiny voice joins in that last chorus.

"SQUEAK, SQUEAK, SQUEAK-SQUEAK-SQUEAK!
SQUEAK, SQUEAK, SQUEAK-SQUEAK-SQUEAK!
SQUEAK, SQUEAK, SQUEAK-SQUEAK-SQUEAK!
SQUEAK-SQUEAK-SQUEAK,
SQUEAK-SQUEAK-SQUEAK-SQUEAK!"

I can't wait for camp to start again!

Sing-Along Suggestions
🐾 🐾 for Og's Songs 🐾 🐾

All of Og's songs can be sung to familiar melodies. Have fun singing!

Pages 5 and 66
Humphrey loves to help his friends .... "Yankee Doodle"

Pages 13, 113 and 132
There was a swamp where lived a frog .... "Bingo"

Page 24
A-camping we will go .... "The Farmer in the Dell"

Pages 42, 59 and 127
What's a Howler? and
Where's the Howler? .... "Frère Jacques"

Page 78
Humphrey's having a journey .... "For He's a Jolly
Good Fellow"

Page 90

Hoppy, hoppy . . . . . "Daisy Bell (Bicycle Built for Two)"

Page 94

Welcome, welcome, to you . . . . . "Happy Birthday to You"

Pages 100 and 107

Hello, Star Frog, how are you? and
Thank you, Star Frog, and bye-bye . . . . "Twinkle, Twinkle,
Little Star"

© Frank Birney

Betty G. Birney has written episodes for numerous children's television shows, including *Madeline, Doug,* and *Bobby's World,* as well as after-school specials and a television movie, *Mary Christmas.* She has won many awards for her television work, including an Emmy, three Humanitas Prizes, and a Writers Guild of America Award.

In addition to the Humphrey books, she is the author of *The Seven Wonders of Sassafras Springs* and *The Princess and the Peabodys.*

A native of St. Louis, Missouri, Betty lives in Los Angeles with her husband, an actor.

Find fun Og and Humphrey activities and teachers' guides at
www.bettygbirney.com
Follow Og, Humphrey and Betty online
www.facebook.com/AccordingtoHumphrey
Twitter: @bettygbirney